37653000583891
Main Fiction: 1st floor
LP WESTERN SLAUGHTER
Deuce

DB	6/14-5/16	
TH	6/16-12/17	
MA	8/18-8/19	
TE	9/19-10/21	
PE	10/21-10/22	

LARGE PRINT

NX 8/09-2/
SLU 6/14-8/16
WESTERN

TH 6/16 - 12/17

DEUCE

Her name was Druscilla Farragut. She was long-legged, handsome, married to a man who drank too much because *he* was married to *her*, and they called her Deuce.

Sheriff Jim Blevins knew as much about her as he needed to know while her hard-drinking husband knew a lot less about her.

It was to be the destiny of Deuce Farragut to enlighten both her husband and Sheriff Blevins in a way which *made* it impossible for either of them to laugh or even smile for a very long time afterwards. Deuce was one hell of a woman.

DEUCE

by

JIM SLAUGHTER

ST. MARTIN'S PRESS
NEW YORK

ROBERT HALE LIMITED
LONDON

© *Robert Hale Ltd. 1979*
First published in Great Britain 1979

ISBN 0 7091 7355 5 *(Standard Edition)*
ISBN 0 7091 7400 4 *(Large Print Edition)*

Robert Hale Limited
Clerkenwell House
Clerkenwell Green
London, EC1R 0HT

St. Martin's Press, Inc.,
175 Fifth Avenue,
New York, N.Y. 10010

ISBN 0–312–19654–7 *(Standard Edition)*
ISBN 0–312–19655–5 *(Large Print Edition)*

Library of Congress Catalog Card Number 78–65945

Printed in Great Britain by
Billing & Sons Limited, Guildford, London and
Worcester

1

ONE LOUSY SHOT!

Sheriff Blevins said, "You take the heart out of a man and you figure he's going to go right on actin' like nothing's happened. Not if he is a man he isn't."

Arnold Ferguson glanced at the big gold watch, then repocketed it and thumped dust from his trousers.

They were all dusty. It had not been a particularly long nor hard ride, but this time of year horsemen scuffed up dust just by staying on the roads.

Ferguson owned the general store across the road northward a few doors. He was a large, ruddy-faced individual, usually thoughtful and circumspect.

But he could become angry and right this minute he was bordering on it.

"Jim, you can't excuse what he did out there."

Sheriff Blevins did not yield. "You know me better'n that, Arnie. I'm just trying to get an idea across, so that when the lynch-talk starts up over at the saloon this evening you and Harry here can tell them it won't solve a darned thing. It'll just make things worse."

The third dusty individual was a wiry, pale-eyed cowman named Harry Horton. He now said, "Most folks aren't even going to know we brought him back or that he shot a posseman, until maybe tomorrow. You're gettin' ahead of yourself, Jim."

Ferguson thought differently and so did Jim Blevins, but it was Ferguson who said, "By nightfall, Harry, everyone in town will know, and so will the cow outfits which aren't more'n a couple miles out. Come along; we still got to take care of the horses."

Sheriff Blevins went to the door with them. He concentrated on Arnold Ferguson. "Talk it down. Tell them I'll be over here with a rack of rifles and loaded scatterguns." When Ferguson looked back and nodded, Blevins also said, "My wife used to say that someday I'd get myself killed over some worthless son of a bitch. Those weren't the exact words but the meaning was the same. I've often thought that if it has to happen I hope it's over someone like Grat Dalton or someone like Frank James—not a guy like Leland Farragut. Hell, his first time out to rob a stage, the horse goes lame and we corner him in some rocks. What kind of an outlaw do you call that?"

He was smiling and Arnie Ferguson made the same kind of poor smile as he turned to follow Harry on across the walk and out to the rack where their drooping horses patiently stood.

From out there Harry looked back to say, "Jim, it ain't exactly the stage robbery. You know that. What did he get? Six dollars and some guy's gold watch. He shot Buff Rhodes."

"Shooting over our heads to turn us back," retorted Blevins in tones of strong disgust, "and he couldn't even do that very well, he had to wing Buff. Harry, you know that was an accident."

Ferguson had his horse untied so he started southward in the direction of the liverybarn with it. All the conversation under the sun was not going to mitigate the fact that he had a business to run, and right this minute he'd have handed over one hundred dollars in crisp new greenbacks to never have to fork another horse in a damned posse.

Blevins returned to the shade of his office and went to the hanging *olla* for a drink of cold water, then he leaned a moment in the open, barred front-wall window gazing up the pale-hot and dust-scented roadway.

He knew Leland Farragut, and because of that he knew as well as he knew his own name that when Lee fired high like that he was trying to warn them off. Lee had known who they were the minute they rode up towards the rocks.

And of course that had to be the exact moment Buff Rhodes stood tall in his stirrups for a better view on ahead where all they had seen was the lame horse.

Right through the shoulder-gristle neat as a knife. It had spun Buff out of the saddle in a sprawl and for a breathless moment Jim Blevins had thought the bullet had struck Rhodes between the eyes, from the way his head snapped.

They had all been nonplussed, and their subsequent relief that Buff was not dead had been so great they had almost allowed Leland Farragut to escape on foot. But Blevins had ridden far out and around and had been sitting there, hands atop the saddle-horn, when Leland emerged into the open.

"You darned fool," he had told the outlaw. "You winged Buff Rhodes. Now throw the guns down and stand still."

The other riders were converging from different directions. Farragut had dropped his Winchester and his sixgun, and Blevins had been unable to avoid reflecting upon this ignominious end to a trail of crime which had begun and ended the same morning, in a jumble of sun-shimmery boulders beside the stageroad.

Buff Rhodes was up the road at Doctor Colendar's place. Except for that very probably people in the Tanque Verde country would have derisively laughed off the entire affair.

That one lousy shot made all the difference because this was not Indiana nor Iowa, this was Arizona Territory where, recently, lame Al Sieber had caught an Apache named Chugesdeslona making *tizwin*, had cut his throat, had pitched the kicking carcass into the cauldron and had ridden back to report on having successfully eliminated another bootlegger.

It was the same Territory where order had been enforced for more than a generation, purely and simply by guns, and maybe, as some authorities including some army generals said, with the variety of unhomogenous population existing here, there was no other way.

But after fifteen years of it, Jim Blevins knew one additional thing for a fact. Where folks thought only in terms of guns, justified or not, that was their only tool for resolving everything from genuine capital crimes to disputes over fences between neighbours.

Lee Farragut? He was one of the best horse-shoers Jim had ever run across. Jim had no illusions. He knew exactly why he felt as he did about Farragut. Not because the town needed a good blacksmith, but because Farragut had made a commonplace error; he had kept a woman when he shouldn't have; had started drinking more than usual last winter and had turned disagreeable; had progressed steadily in both those areas, drinking and snarling, until this summer. Then he had tried to rob that coach.

He'd had friends once, along the bar and over at the harness works and in the poolhall. Even down in the tree-shade out front of the liverybarn where the whittlers and chewers congregated each day.

That had been about a year back. By this time, today, Lee Farragut had sacrificed them all. People had been moving out of his way for six months now and Jim had wondered how long it would be before he and Lee tangled.

He had not imagined it would be under these circumstances, although Jim was in some ways dolorous enough to have expected something about like this. Living alone, Doc Colendar had once told him, did that to men; made them unsmiling. Jim's retort had been, "John; fifteen years at my trade and you'd have a hell of a time scraping up a smile too."

But that was only part of it, and maybe not even the biggest part. They had told him back at Omaha a hot, dry climate was his wife's only chance, and hell, she'd died within a year after setting up housekeeping here in Muletown.

James Blevins knew something about what a woman meant in a man's life. A good one or a bad one, it didn't make a whole lot of difference providing the man had the kind of depth to him which made love as much of his day-to-day existence as breathing.

This was what lay behind his thoughts about Leland Farragut. Would unmarried Harry Horton who lived out of his hat in the manzanita brakes south-west of town ever understand? Or Arnold Ferguson who had never been married? Or Buffie Rhodes whose knowledge—and experience—with women was limited to excursions over to Springville to visit Squirrel-Tooth Annie's 'Palace of Pleasure'? Hell; that was like seeking virtue by turning the devil into a corralful of crippled saints; it made just about that much sense.

Blevins hitched up off the adobe sill and started to turn back for another drink at the *olla* when someone over in front of the Mex cafe sang out to a pair of bronzed horsemen walking their animals up through from the lower end of town.

"Hey! You hear about the southbound stage gettin' robbed north of town this morning?"

Evidently the riders had not heard because they reined over towards the cafe and that loud rangeman standing there.

"You fellers would never guess who it was. You know that shoeing-shed north of the liverybarn? ... Yeah, by golly, that's him—Farragut. How's that for a surprise?"

It must have been a surprise indeed because one of the cowboys made a high whistling sound and his friend sat there wagging his head.

Blevins turned away from the *olla*, grabbed his big brass ring and went over to unlock the cell-room door. It was cooler down in there but it was also less lighted and had a mouldy smell. The jailhouse walls were four feet thick and the ceilings were not quite seven feet high. At one time, so legend had it, the Muletown jailhouse had been an *alcalde's* residence and out back where the cedar posts still stood had been both a stock and a gibbet. The *alcaldes* back in the days of Mexican sovereignty had possessed a lot of power. More for a fact than any single low-level *americano* official had.

If the jailhouse had indeed been a residence it did not speak highly for the residences back in those days. Only because Jim Blevins had personally bought the material and had done the work was there a wooden floor in his front office. Otherwise, back there in the cell-room it was still an earthen floor, packed as hard as granite.

And for that matter, the name of the town was not Muletown. Or maybe it was now, because at both entrances, from the north and the south, someone had put up signs announcing that 'Muletown' had a population of three hundred people. On those signs it was spelled right out

M-u-l-e-t-o-w-n, but the town's name was Montazgo, meaning in Spanish a place where people had to pay a toll when moving cattle from one province to another. In those days Montazgo had been part of a Mexican province, and south of it had been the other Mex provinces.

People had always encountered difficulty spelling the proper name, and more trouble pronouncing it, so, through simple attrition the name had evolved into 'Muletown' which was by and large acceptable, except to the people over in Mex town, and they thought it was hilarious what the *gringos* had made out of a simple word such as Montazgo. They also thought it demonstrated what crude people the owners of their ancestral countryside were.

But they were not sufficiently flawless to cast the first stone. Muletown had in its earlier days been one of those border communities which throve upon cattle and horse theft. And that was for a hundred years before any *gringos* arrived there.

Otherwise, probably, that stock and gibbet would not have been erected out behind the *alcalde's* residence.

From the cell Jim Blevins had locked his prisoner in the leaning old unused gibbet was clearly visible. It had been deliberately left standing, the idea being that if prisoners had to look out there long enough, that frightening old grim object would do a lot more towards cleansing their hearts and souls, than a courtroom trial would do.

Maybe. Maybe not.

2

THE LITTLE SCALE

Leland Farragut was a lanky man, big-boned and heavier than he appeared to be. He gazed stonily out where Jim Blevins came to rest in the little musty corridor and said, "How's Buff?"

Blevins had not been down to the doctor's cottage yet. "Madder'n a hop-toad the last I knew. Why didn't you elevate the barrel before you fired?"

"I did!"

"Not enough, Lee."

"And everyone's mad now."

Blevins considered the tall man inside those steel straps which made up the cage. "What have you done lately that was *right* ?"

"Is that why you came down here—
to rag me?"

"No. To tell you that shooting Buff
Rhodes makes a lot of difference. You
know what I'm talking about?"

"I could be tried for attemptin' to
murder someone?"

Jim shook his head. "I'm talking
about the history for lynchings they
got here in Muletown."

The prisoner turned to fully face
Sheriff Blevins with the bars between
them. He did not open his mouth, he
just stared.

Blevins did not have to articulate.
Leland Farragut had lived in the Tanque Verde countryside even longer
than Blevins had. For all Jim knew,
Farragut could even have been one of
those nameless and faceless individuals
who from time to time in the past had
leaned on hang-ropes.

Finally the prisoner said, "Buff
didn't die."

Jim did not even bother answering

that. They both knew perfectly well that a man did not have to die for an outlaw to be lynched for a shooting, all a man had to do was get himself shot by a lawbreaker, nor was that an exclusive south-desert custom, either.

Blevins said, "You expecting a visitor, Lee?"

Farragut's troubled, steady gaze drew out narrower. "You're talking about Deuce?"

Blevins again ignored a question and stood awaiting his answer. Farragut moved from the window to the wall-bunk and sank down fishing for his tobacco and papers. He had his shadowed face tipped forward so that even his profile was not very visible in the gloomy cell-room.

"Have you seen her?" he asked Blevins, elaborately working up a cigarette as though nothing on earth was as important to him as that smoke. "Has she been around, Jim?"

"No," replied Blevins, with more

emphasis than had been necessary. "And I haven't seen her. And I don't aim to go hunt her up, either."

"By now she knows where I am and what happened," stated the slumped figure in the shadows as cigarette smoke curled fragrantly upwards. "She'll be along. You can't expect a decent woman to sashay right down here in broad daylight and walk into a jailhouse."

Blevins looked away. Decent woman! He looked back as he said, "Lee, you are a damned fool, a stupid bastard and a plain idiot." He paused to pull down a fresh breath.

The man on the wall-bunk went right on smoking and gazing dead ahead as though there were no one within ten miles of him. A moment later, though, as Jim started to turn away, his prisoner made a comment.

"Yeah, I know. Jim; she come from a place where womenfolk got lacy underthings, and cameos on their velvet chokers. Back there she even had her own driving rig and a nice chestnut mare. She showed me pictures of them. And of her with friends dressed like a queen."

The lanky big man arose, crossed his cell in three strides and turned to cross back. He looked out into the corridor. "You ever know a horse-shoer who could give his woman stuff like that?"

Blevins sounded exasperated when he replied. "I never knew a hard-luck outlaw who could do it either, Leland."

"She deserves them things."

They exchanged a long look and Blevins had to swallow hard to keep from saying what he was thinking. He probably would never have said it except that Farragut moved closer to the front of the cell and put a cold look of menace upon Blevins.

"She deserves things and I'm going to get them for her."

"How—from the inside of this

darned cell? Lee for gawd's sake listen
to me!"

"You say one bad word about my
wife, Sheriff, and when I get out of
here I'll bust your head like a rotten
pumpkin! I know you don't like her.
She knows it too and she's told me
you'd run her out of town if she wasn't
my wife. Take my word for it, Jim,
you say one thing——"

"Leland; I don't have to say it,
everyone else already has. Listen to
me; I don't think you're going to get
out of here."

"I am entitled to a trial by gawd."

"Lee, that's what I'm trying to get
across to you. For shooting a lawman
in the performance of his duty——"

"What *law*man for Chris'sake?
Buffie Rhodes rides for a living, he's
no lawman!"

"He became one the minute I swore
him in and handed him the badge,
Lee. My point is, when you winged
Buff Rhodes you shot a lawman. You

been in the Territory longer than I have. You'd ought to know what happens. If you don't get lynched, when you stand trial you could damned well end up in prison."

Farragut dropped his cigarette and ground it to death underfoot. "Is this what you come down here to do—try and scare me?"

Blevins gave up. "Naw. Forget it, Lee." He started to turn back.

"Wait a minute." The lanky man went over and gripped the bars. "My wife deserves to know what's going on." He paused, took a fresh grip and in a slightly different tone said, "Jim, go talk with her. Just don't scare her. I'm asking this as an old friend. Just go and set with her for a while, she worries——"

Blevins woodenly nodded and walked back up out of the cell-room, locked the oaken door, tossed his brass key-ring atop the desk and said a fierce word out loud.

"Yeah, she worries. Sweet, innocent, trusting little Deuce Farragut worries. The same way a gila monster or a sidewinder worries, and maybe even about the same things—nothing but herself."

He grabbed a hat from the wallrack, took another long pull at the *olla*, spilled the old hat upon the back of his head and went outside to turn and securely lock the steel-reinforced oak door after himself.

Across the road out front of the harness works several loafing townsmen watched, and up the road a short distance, out front of the poolhall, three rangeriders looked on without comment, their hatbrim-shaded lean faces expressionless.

Blevins walked up as far as the small residence with the white fence out front and turned in through the picket gate where a shingle nailed to a post said 'John J. Colendar, M.D.'

Doctor Colendar's residence had

four rooms in front to be used in conjunction with his trade. Two were bedrooms for ill people, one was an examination room, and the one he was emerging from, unlit cigar clamped between his teeth, as Sheriff Blevins walked in, was his office.

Doctor Colendar was a man of average height, a widower like Jim Blevins was, greying up the side of his head over each temple, and dead level in the way he looked at people. As Blevins turned to close the door after himself the medical practitioner removed his cold cigar and pointed towards a closed door.

"Buff's in there if you want to see him, but it'd be better if you waited until tomorrow."

Blevins raised enquiring eyebrows.

"Well, confound it, he was shot wasn't he?" stated the doctor. "The loss of blood alone was serious. And the shock was probably even more serious to his system. He's not going to die, but for a while he's not going to do any fandangos either. Jim; he needs lots of sleep, lots of rest. By the way—right now he's asleep so unless what you got to say is very important I'd appreciate it if you stayed out of there."

Blevins had nothing in particular to say to Buff Rhodes. He'd just been interested in his progress.

Doctor Colendar said, "You got a match on you?" and when Jim shook his head the doctor turned away with a mild curse and a harsh judgement. "Hell! The trouble with you folks who've quit tobacco is that you don't seem to realise matches are part of every man's personal equipment. You can clean your ears with them, light stoves and fireplaces with them, even use them ... Come in here for a minute, Jim——"

The doctor found a match in the examination room, lit his cigar then went over and fished in a small metal tray with a pair of tweezers, picked up something, turned and said, "Hold out your hand."

He dropped a flattened lead bullet upon the sheriff's palm.

Blevins made a cursory examination. Whatever that little mis-shapen piece of lead had struck had undoubtedly been very hard because the lead was so flattened and warped it was not even possible to make certain it had once been a bullet, except for the two ridges, one above the other, where a brass casing had been crimped around it.

Jim looked up. "Out of Buff?"

"Yes. You thought it had gone all the way through, didn't you?"

Blevins had indeed thought that. "There was the hole in front where it hit him, John, and there was a hole with blood around it out back."

Colendar said, "Ah hah! You see what jumping to conclusions can get you into? That hole in back was made by a piece of bone not by an exiting bullet. That there slug was stopped cold on the inside of his collarbone, and if the idiot had been a few yards closer, it *and* some more bone, might very well have busted out the back."

Doctor Colendar removed his cigar, examined the unevenly forming grey ash, stepped to a wastebasket along the wall, dropped ash over there and came back as Sheriff Blevins moved to pick up a magnifying glass lying upon the examination table.

Colendar said, "It's a bullet, you can take my word for it. I've taken out my share of those things from live ones and dead ones."

Blevins continued to turn the slug and peer through at it. Then he lay aside the glass, considered Doc's little precision scales and said, "Weigh this thing for me, Doc."

Colendar came over, placed the slug upon one of the round elements and bent over to read the sliding gauge.

While he did that Sheriff Blevins removed a .45 cartridge from his shellbelt, picked up a pair of pliers and was about to extract the bullet when Colendar saw, and with a lunge grabbed back the little pliers.

"You know how hard it is to get a pair of surgical nippers out here!" he irately demanded, and pocketed the tool lest the sheriff get it again, and went to a drawer at the far end of the room, returned and handed Blevins a regular pair of pliers. "What are you trying to do?"

Blevins worked the slug out of his .45 casing as he said, "I'm not sure, John." He held out the bullet. "Weigh this one for me too, will you?"

Colendar went over and leaned down to perform the same ritual again. He grunted, jiggled the scale and weighed the second bullet.

Behind him Sheriff Blevins said, "Much difference?"

"Quite a bit, Jim, quite a bit."

"John, when you dug that flat one out of Buff, did you get all of it?"

Colendar straightened up frowning. "Every shred. There was no shattering as you can see. Nor did the bullet break up. It just struck and flattened, and I'd say it had lost most of its momentum when it hit Buff because it did not really plough through as one might normally assume a .45 slug would do."

"That's my point," stated Jim Blevins, reaching for both slugs. "It's not a .45 bullet, John. When you dropped it in my hand it seemed too light, and by golly it *is* too light."

Colendar puffed, then removed his cigar. "All right. It's not a .45 slug. What of it?"

"Leland was carrying a Winchester saddlegun, which he did not use, and his Colt sixgun."

Colendar turned that over in his mind for a moment, eyebrows slowly converging above quizzical eyes. "Spell it out, will you?"

"Yeah. How could Leland have shot Buff Rhodes off his horse like he did, unless he had shot either his saddlegun or his beltgun?"

"How would I know? You're the lawman."

"He couldn't have, John."

"He had a hide-out weapon——"

"No he didn't. I went over him before we brought him back. I put everything in his hat—money, watch, pocketknife, and he didn't have another weapon." They looked at one another, then because the only ready solution Blevins could imagine was the one which had occurred to him earlier, he asked again if it were possible that a piece of that flattened bullet had either emerged or was still inside Buff Rhodes.

Colendar, who was not a man to dismiss even unthinking reflections upon his skill, waited a moment before replying.

"That is the entire slug, Jim. I did *not* miss any of it. Take it down the street and have the gunsmith tell you whether any of it is missing or not. I can tell you right now, and I'm no authority on guns, that this is all there was of that bullet." Colendar waited, then said, "I'm brewing coffee in the kitchen, care for any?" He waited a reasonable time for an answer then raised his voice. "*Jim!* Do you want a cup of java with me?"

Blevins shook his head, muttered, "Thanks, John," and walked out through the cottage and into the sunshine out front.

The only even remotely rational explanation he could imagine was that, for some reason, Leland Farragut had not had full-size forty-five slugs in his bullet-casings, and that made about as much sense as pounding sand in a rathole.

He did not visit the gunsmith, he went on back to his jailhouse office, brought out Farragut's sixgun and meticulously examined every slug in the gun as well as in the shellbelt. Every one of them was a .45 bullet.

He put the outlaw's gun away, delved through his desk for a sack of tobacco and some wheatstraw papers and sat down to solemnly roll and light a smoke. He had not, as Doctor Colendar had said, stopped smoking altogether, he had simply given up doing it steadily.

Special occasions warranted a special smoke.

After sifting through at least a dozen ideas he turned back to the second or third one and blew smoke at the fly-specked ceiling while expanding on this one. Then he glanced out the window. The afternoon was advancing. Within another couple of hours it would be dark. What he had in mind would now have to wait until morning.

He finished the smoke, went across to the Mex cafe for two big bowls of carne con chili, *which was how Mexicans said* chili con carne, brought them back and left one on his desk while taking the second one down to Leland Farragut.

He did not say a word. Not even when Leland asked if Jim had gone to talk to Leland's wife. He just shook his head, turned and went back up to the office.

The last thing he did, a couple of hours later, before barring himself inside for the night, was go study the sky for any signs of clouds.

There were no clouds, for even though this was autumn on the south desert, the rains normally did not arrive until after December.

3

A LITTLE LIGHTNING

Her name was Druscilla, but ever since she had been around the Tanque Verde country people who knew her well enough to use a nickname had called her Deuce. That was what her husband called her.

She was tall, a shade over five feet and seven inches and that was without the heels on her riding boots. With the boots on, Sheriff Blevins who was an even six feet tall, could just about meet her grey eyes on a dead-level.

She was a handsome woman, probably close to thirty or perhaps even a little beyond. She was leggy and small-waisted but where most leggy females were lean and lithe, Deuce was firm-busted and when she walked away men stared.

What Jim Blevins knew about Deuce Farragut was enough. He did not like her. What she had surmised and had told Leland about Blevins was Gospel truth. If Jim could have legally run her out of Muletown he would have done it.

But as he stood now looking at her on the porch of the horse-shoer's cottage over behind the shoeing-shed along the southern end of town, he admitted to himself that she looked like one hell of a female-woman.

And *that* was what underlay what he knew about her.

She had listened to all he had woodenly recounted, and at the conclusion she had wagged her head wearing a crooked small mirthless smile.

"The horse lamed up. My gawd wouldn't you just know it. With anyone else they'd ride off with a bullion box. With that husband of mine—the damned horse went lame." She looked at Blevins. "Why did he shoot Buffie?"

"Accident. Meant to fire over our heads and spook us."

"Accident? Shooting in the air and hitting someone?"

"He didn't tip up the barrel enough, Deuce."

She rolled her eyes heavenward with a look of forlorn resignation. Then she looked at Blevins and said, "Then what? I mean, what happens to him now?"

"Trial when the circuit rider gets back here."

"What will he get? Five years at Yuma prison maybe?"

Blevins tactfully avoided that one by saying, "I only bring them in and arraign them. The rest of it's up to the judge. I can't even say which judge it'll be. There are four of them on the circuit." He and the busty tall woman looked at one another with mutual but veiled antipathy. He had a question for her.

"By any chance do you want to sell the grulla horse Leland bought for you a couple of years back?"

Her eyes widened. "Sell him? I never thought of it, Sheriff. Why; you need another saddle animal?"

"Yeah. And I always liked that one. Where is he?"

"Out back in the shed." She studied his face then turned to move towards the door. "I'll think about it and maybe I might just up and sell him to you at that."

A few moments later Jim left walking northward. He made a complete sashay up as far as the north end of town, paused up there for a while studying the length of Main Street, then walked westward to the entrance to the back-alley and started down through there.

People had been leaving litter in the

alley for so long it was hazardous to walk down through there almost any time of the day, but Jim Blevins had no difficulty until he was within sight of the liverybarn's alley-exit at the lower end of town, then he encountered a black dog with a two-foot-long bony tail, and while the dog hardly qualified as litter, he had watched Blevins coming along and had made up his mind that Blevins was not to go past.

He was a rangy, tall dog, mostly black but with some cinnamon colouring on his undersides. He got up, stretched, then deliberately walked out to block the sheriff's onward course. Blevins had been bitten by his share of dogs. He read this one's stance correctly and growled a curse. The black dog did did not budge. He spoke more sharply and instinctively hauled his hand back to let it lie on the saw-handle grip of his holstered Colt. The black dog was not the slightest bit intimidated although he should have been.

Blevins got within ten feet and halted. Beyond, to his left through a stand of tall, summer-cured stickery weeds was the Farragut horse-shed.

A hostler came forth from down by the liverybarn pushing a laden manure barrow. He looked up, took in the scene at once, dropped his barrow and started up there. From a fair distance he said, "Don't shoot him, Sheriff. He don't mean nothin'." The hostler walked up, grabbed the black dog and with a fierce jerk dragged him away.

Blevins did not know that particular hostler, but that was not surprising, they came and went like flies. Mostly, their problem was that they drank. For some reason that affliction seemed to plague liverymen. The hired kind anyway.

Blevins went over into thin shade by the Farragut rear fence and casually looked all around. Then he slipped through and got inside the horse-shed. The horse dozing in there was docile, but being startled from a doze would have no doubt changed that if Blevins hadn't talked his way right on up, laid a hand on the grulla gelding, talked quietly, petted him, then worked his way down and lifted a foot.

The shoe was worn but a perfect fit. He went completely around with all four hooves, patted the grulla again and slipped back to the alley. From there it was only a short distance on down to the liverybarn where he again encountered the bony-tailed big black dog, only now he wagged his tail and grinned.

Blevins walked to the middle of the runway, saw the dayman and called for his private mount to be brought out, then he went to the harness room for his outfit.

There were stem-winding blue-tailed flies in the runway. No matter how hard liverymen worked to keep their places of business clean and fly-free, they never entirely succeeded. Maybe it was the nature of their business, because for a fact neither the gunsmith nor the harness-maker had that trouble with flies. Not even this time of year on the south desert.

Blevins rode out of town on the north stageroad with a fresh sun off to his right. The day showed promise of being a little cooler than its predecessors, and that would be pleasant. In fact it was that time of year; even on the south desert, summer had to make some concessions otherwise the life-giving rain would never arrive, sparse as it was, and of course that would end it for four-legged as well as two-legged life down there. As things were, the south desert was a marginally inhabitable place, and as Jim Blevins rode up through the gentle morning he marvelled at the fragile beauty of this area where most people could not leave fast enough.

You either liked the south desert or you did not like it. If there was an in-between sentiment about it Blevins had never encountered it. Also, the people who lived down there and presumably did so from choice and who therefore liked it, could count on the return each springtime of a kind of natural beauty found no place else on earth, and which only lasted one breathless month before heat came to wither it all for another year.

He looked out over the autumn landscape now towards the blurred far mountains and smiled in recollection at the way his wife had loved springtime in this country. He thanked God she'd been able to stay long enough to experience a south desert springtime.

His reverie ended when he saw the jumble of big old grey boulders on his left. They were still a good mile ahead, but in the winy air of this kind of morning they seemed less than a third of that distance onward.

He left the coachroad and skirted completely around the boulder field, then rode back about to the place where he had met Leland Farragut emerging from the boulders, swung to earth, tethered his horse to a flourishing catclaw bush and went ahead on foot.

He found it almost at once; less in fact than two hundred feet ahead into the maze of rocks—that second set of bootprints he had suspected might be out here.

He shook his head and softly swore.

When Leland had tried to escape by walking out of here, Jim had anticipated it and had thought how clever he was to guess where the outlaw would emerge and to face Leland over there.

Clever? He had been a damned idiot, that's what it had amounted to. Leland had walked out like that with the deliberate intention of being caught.

Why? There were the tracks; smaller than man-tracks and narrower, and they did not sink far enough into the dusty old soil to have been created by anyone carrying much weight.

Blevins lifted his hat, scratched, went over to sit upon a big round rock and gaze steadily over where that second set of tracks came, and went.

"Deuce," he said aloud in disgust. "Blevins, you simple-minded horse's rearend, they caught you out and you never even rode on down through here to look around. If you had, you'd have found her hiding in those darned rocks ... Well; maybe she'd had nailed you too." He pushed up off the rock and walked almost indifferently back and forth following her boot-marks.

Of course there was no natural law which declared those marks had to have been made by Deuce Farragut, but Leland Farragut would never have been caught dead up here or anywhere else for that matter, with anyone but Deuce.

Several things made more sense to Jim now than they had made yesterday. One of them was that robbery itself. Lee was a fool, had been drinking too much lately, and was troublesome—but if he was outlaw-material Jim Blevins would eat his hat.

But that damned woman of his was something different, and while Jim's ability to judge men was excellent and he had never even thought of himself as being qualified to do the same for womenfolk, he had no misgivings about his earliest judgement of Deuce Farragut being incorrect. He had known a hundred men who had the same character—cold, calculating, totally self-centred, maybe even deadly, but certainly capable of using a fool like Lee, and also evidently capable of aiming squarely at a posseman to halt the oncoming horsemen long enough to hide herself and to encourage her stupid husband to give himself up and to divert the possemen from searching the rocks.

Possemen? No; keeping *Jim Blevins* from searching the rocks.

One thing puzzled him. He found the tracks of only one horse. He walked around in that boulder-field of huge stones and until he went beyond it, north-westerly where there was a stand of lacy paloverdes, he did not locate what he sought. Then he did, and the horse which had been tied over there had worn the same size shoes as Deuce's grulla wore; shoes which were in the exact same stage of wear.

Blevins stood looking elsewhere. The sun was climbing and now, finally, the heat was rolling in again. Even so it was not going to be oppressive. Probably for the balance of the year it would not be that way again.

He wished for a smoke and instead

turned back walking slowly towards the place where he had left his horse.

As for the bullet, he had suspected almost at once, right after John Colendar had weighed the slug, permitting Blevins to make an accurate comparison.

The reason he had suspected her was because upon a number of occasions he had seen Deuce Farragut return from riding out over the desert wearing a Colt Lightning, the only sidearm Colt made which fired that light a bullet.

The rest of it had been gut-feeling. He was willing to admit it was also in part based upon his dislike of her and his willingness to believe something like this about her.

But it still had not occurred to him yesterday when he had been out here with his posse that Leland Farragut had anyone in those cursed rocks with him, and *that* was going to come back to haunt Jim as a lawman for a long time.

Even if he had wanted to conceal the fact that he had only half done his job yesterday this was one of those situations, with everyone taking a concerted interest in it, which would ultimately be dissected detail by detail.

Well; the hell with the future, right now he had to get back to work on the present.

He snugged up his cincha, stepped across leather and turned back towards town. What he had to do now, of course, was prove that she had been in those rocks with her husband. The horsetracks he knew from long experience were very unreliable pieces of evidence.

The rest of what he had to use in working up a warrant for her arrest was no better. There were a lot of Lightning Colts around. But the worst part of it was that when he'd been out there with his possemen, and she'd successfully hidden in the rocks, he'd lost his best opportunity not only to apprehend her, but to later on be able to call as witnesses such men as Harry Horton and Arnold Ferguson, men of substance in the area.

A rattling old faded stagecoach coming south from up around Indian Wells and Fort Advance scuffed great pennants of dun dust as it hastened towards Muletown. The driver and gunguard no doubt saw Blevins off to the west riding in roughly the same direction. They may also have already learned of the robbery because although they normally would have waved to anyone they met, this time neither man so much as raised a gauntleted hand and the pace was picked up for a half-mile or so, until they were well beyond where Blevins would finally reach the roadway.

He took his time. There probably was no reason for him not to.

Muletown was one of those places where trouble did not ever seem to arrive with much of a vengeance. An old man who years ago, when Blevins had first arrived in the country, had said it was just plain too hot most of the time for folks to get worked up about things, could have been right.

It had been said facetiously, but maybe there was a lick of truth in it.

He entered town from over on the west side and left his animal for the dayman at the liverybarn to look after. He went up to his office, drank, unlocked the cell-room door and was greeted by a searing blast of profanity from a prisoner who had missed a meal and was not at all happy about it.

Jim braced into the tirade and remained standing silently beyond the steel doorway until it had subsided, then he said, "You're an even bigger damnfool than I thought you were, Lee. She didn't just make a fool out of me yesterday, she made an even bigger one out of you. She'll likely never come to trial for being out there with you—supervising things if I got her pegged right—unless you sign a statement saying she was with you."

"What are you saying," exclaimed Farragut in disdain. "I was alone out there."

"Naw you weren't. I saw her tracks and the tracks of her horse."

"You went out there this morning?"

"Just got back. Leland, she made me look like a schoolkid but you're coming out even worse. You're going to go to prison sure as I'm standing here, unless they lynch you first."

Farragut pulled out his makings, squinted at the little sack and as he went to work manufacturing a smoke he said, "Fetch me some more tobacco when you go after my dinner … Jim; I'd no more tell you she was in them rocks with me than I'd fly to the moon." He lit up and turned, looking through the bars with smoke trickling from his lips. "I doubt that you can do anything about them tracks."

Blevins inclined his head a little. "I probably can't. By the time a circuit rider gets here they won't even be out there any more."

"So you figure to force me into signing a paper against her?"

Jim sighed and shook his head. He knew Farragut better than to even consider such a thing. He would not sign any such paper if he were dragged behind wild horses.

"Naw," stated Blevins. "Lee, all I wanted to do was tell you she made a fool out of both of us. But with me, I'll still be free to go and come as I like."

Farragut smoked and seemed to be thinking of something, then he turned his back and went over to the recessed long, very narrow window to lean and gaze out where sunshine reflected off the ancient gibbet.

Blevins returned to the front office,

locked the cell-room door as he always did when there was a prisoner down there, got another drink from the *olla* then decided to stroll up and see how Buff Rhodes was today.

As for Deuce Farragut, he would get her and nail her hide to the wall. He had no idea how he could do that, but he had the doggedly unyielding stubbornness which kept him thinking that he would to it—somehow.

Outside, the town seemed somnolent as it always did this late in the day. Those clouds which yesterday had peeped from behind the far-away hills were no longer in sight. If there had been a little storm on the way, it had evidently got sidetracked.

4

A MATTER OF BEER

Buff Rhodes was about thirty, give or take a year, and looked to be exactly what he was, a professional rangeman. He had blue eyes, sandy hair which was sunburnt, and a round, tanned face except up across the forehead where the skin was the colour of a snake's undersides from always being protected by a hat.

When Jim Blevins walked in Buff was reading a newspaper. He put it aside, studied Jim's face a moment, then said, "Me'n Doc been talking about that darned fool hitting me by mistake. Sheriff, it just don't make sense to me. No cowboy I ever seen was that poor a shot."

Jim shrugged. "How you feeling?"

"Like someone who's been shot. I couldn't be luckier though. I'm sure grateful for all Doc's done. Hey; what about Farragut?"

"He's in a cell. There'll be a hearing when the circuit rider shows up ... Buff, when you rose up in the stirrups to look over yonder into the rocks, what did you see?"

"See? I didn't see a darned thing before Leland shot me. I didn't even see Leland. Now I got a question for you. Some of the fellers come around this morning ... Tell me straight out, Sheriff, if there was a lynching would you get in the way?"

"With shotguns primed with lead slugs and every other weapon I could lay hands on, Buff. Who were these fellers who came to talk to you this morning?"

Rhodes looked disgusted. "Don't expect I have to tell you. How's come you don't just let 'em take Leland out and hang him? Think how much money it'd save for the Territory. And he's as guilty as they come."

Blevins sat gazing at the young cowboy. It would have been so easy—and personally satisfying—to tell Buff he didn't know what he was talking about; that Farragut was *not* guilty.

Doctor Colendar walked in and halted in the doorway surprised to see who Buff's visitor was. He said, "I thought it was Clint and Burr again."

Buff got a startled expression on his face and swiftly looked at the sheriff. Blevins was gently smiling. "I'll look them up and have a little discussion with them about lynchings," he said, and arose to turn towards John Colendar. "I'd like a word with you," he said, escorting the medical practitioner out into the little ante-room and closing Buff's door behind them.

"John, don't mention to anyone that we figured out the slug from Rhodes was not a forty-five."

Doctor Colendar was perfectly agreeable. "Suits me. I think I can guess the rest of it, Jim. He had someone with him up there in the rocks?"

"Yeah, but so far only you and me and Leland know it, and I'd like to have things stay that way for a spell."

Colendar considered the lawman's rugged, bronzed countenance briefly then said, "What did he look so worried for when I mentioned his partners visiting him this morning? They got a hand in the robbery too?"

"Not in the robbery. They were talking up a lynch party with him and he didn't want me to know their names, and you walked in dropping names one after the other." Blevins grinned. "If those two are still over at the saloon I'd ought to be able to scare a big five-cent stein of beer out of them."

He and Doctor Colendar laughed, then Blevins returned to the roadway, and the last thing John Colendar said was: "It may not be a joke."

Blevins nodded and walked away. He knew better than anyone that lynching Leland Farragut might not be a joke. But he was going to treat it like one if he could.

The saloon in the early afternoon was not a very busy place, but when Blevins walked in from the sunshine two cowboys at the bar saw him and exchanged a look, then one pulled his hat rim low and said, "Let's get on back," and started for the door.

Blevins allowed them to get almost over there, then he caught the tallest and youngest one with a crooked arm and whirled him back. "Burr, did anyone ever explain to you what the penalty is for interferin' with a lawman in the performance of his duty?"

The lanky cowboy paled and looked away, looked at his companion.

"If it's a jail-break you get involved in," went on the sheriff. "There's a hell of a possibility that you'll get shot and killed. But if that don't happen, you'll be more of a fugitive than Farragut is."

The second rangerider blustered at Blevins. "What the hell's botherin' you anyway, Sheriff? All's we done was ride in today and have a few——"

"And try to talk up a lynching," interjected Blevins, took his hand off Burr's arm and jerked his head. "Stay out of town for three weeks, gents."

"For three ...! You can't make no order like that," the shorter of the duo cried.

"I can arrest you right now, Clint, and when you shoot off your mouth like you're doing, I can cite you on that for resisting." Jim paused, then jerked a thumb towards the doors. "And don't come back for three weeks, either one of you. And one more word about lynching someone and I'll come after you. *Get!*"

The shorter one might have argued,

he seemed argumentative by nature, but the lanky one gave him a rough push and kept on pushing until they were outside.

Blevins heard the argument start up out there and turned to find the barman interestedly watching him while at the same time he polished glasses.

The bar was deserted. There were four old men playing cards, whist probably, over near a corner window. The building could have caught afire and they would not have noticed.

The barman drew off a beer and slid it down. He then followed it to say, "Them boys was just tellin' me how Buff Rhodes didn't look none too good, Sheriff."

Blevins drank first, then said, "Them boys is liars, friend. I just came from Doc's place and Rhodes looked better than he looked *before* he was shot. At least Doc made him take a bath."

"Well, why would them boys tell me a lie?"

"Because, *amigo*, they were trying to talk up a lynching. You can't hope to bust someone out of jailhouse as thick-walled as mine unless you've got a lot of men to help."

The barman shifted his glance, coloured, and when Jim put his five-cent piece atop the bar for the beer, the bartender refused to touch it.

"Hell, Sheriff, that one's on the house."

Blevins watched the barman walk away, thinking how inexpensive the man's conscience was. It could be cleansed for a five-cent piece.

Blevins was not much of a drinker any more than he was much of a smoker or chewer. Nonetheless this particular beer was very tasty so he slowly savoured it. The reason it was such a welcome thing was because it had not cost anything. That had to be the reason because every glass of suds served in this place came from the same cask.

Arnie Ferguson walked in wearing his storekeeper's apron, but tucked up a little so he could walk faster. He hoisted a box to the bartop, said, "That's the order," to the barman, then turned to face the sheriff. "Heard something this afternoon that might interest you Jim. The circuit rider was over at Springville until this morning, then he left riding in this direction."

It did indeed interest Blevins. He got expansive and offered to buy Ferguson a beer, but it was a safe offer, Ferguson did not drink at all and everyone including the sheriff, knew it.

"They tell me there's one of those circuit-riders who heaves the book at them," stated the storekeeper. "I hope this here is the one."

Jim was not too interested one way or another. The law was spelled out, along with the degrees of punishment, for robbing stages. A lenient judge could bend a point or two but he could not do much more. And when a felonious armed assault was involved ... "Sure you won't have that beer?" asked Jim, turning slightly towards the storekeeper.

"You know blasted well I don't touch any kind of liquor," exclaimed the annoyed merchant.

Blevins was unperturbed. "Just being polite is all."

"You're just darned sure you won't have to buy me a beer," Ferguson said, turning as the barman sauntered up with some greenbacks and passed them over. Evidently whatever Ferguson had brought around in that box had been expensive. Blevins said, "Well then, Arnie, *you* can buy *me* one."

Ferguson turned swiftly as he stuffed the greenbacks into a pocket. "Not on your life. If you want to ruin your insides and become degraded and debauched, that is your business, but

I'll never have it on my conscience I was a party to the ruination——"

"All right, all right," stated the sheriff, breaking in by raising his voice. "Arnie, I marvel that you set foot inside this nest of vipers, this den of iniquity."

Ferguson was really upset by this time, and he was preparing to depart but had to get in one last broadside. "I wouldn't have set foot in here if they'd agreed to come down to the store. I got plenty of business without saloon-business. Deuce Farragut was just in buying a whole wheelbarrow load of groceries. And two of the cow outfits got wagons out back at the dock!"

Ferguson got across the room and out the door before Sheriff Blevins finished his beer and turned to also hasten out of the saloon.

The lanky bartender gazed at his roadside doors and waggled his head. Still, in his trade there were all kinds, and usually, even sometimes in the middle of the week, you got them all in one day.

Sheriff Blevins caught up with Ferguson in the doorway of the gunshop which was two doors north of the general store. He caught the merchant's arm and hauled him around. Ferguson wrenched his arm free. He was red in the face, and clearly Arnold Ferguson was one of those people who continued to increase the height of their anger even after whatever had bothered them was no longer really relevant.

"Arnie, you said Leland's wife bought a barrow-load of stuff."

"What of it!"

"Exactly what kind of stuff?"

"Well now, what do womanfolk buy in a general store—tinned peaches—I got some dented tins and they go a little cheaper—tinned beef, quite a slug of that, some spuds—they're grown over in Mex town, very good potatoes at that—and some flour and baking soda, some tobacco and corn and Mex oranges from below the line." Ferguson stopped and stood staring at Blevins. "What's this all about; since when do you care what Deuce Farragut buys in the way of supplies?"

"Just since we locked up her husband," stated Blevins quietly. "She don't smoke, Arnie."

"Well, I know that. Still and all, maybe she's figurin' on taking the tobacco to Leland over in your cell-room."

"Yeah, maybe," conceded Jim Blevins, and smiled. "Sorry I got to teasing you up there." He nodded and struck out on a diagonal course for the jailhouse. Ferguson looked after him and did the identical thing that lanky barman had done, he irritably shook his head.

When Leland Farragut heard Blevins up in the office he bellowed and rattled the door of his cell. Jim did not

even open the door and ask, he knew
what Farragut wanted so he went back
across the road to the Mex cafe, got a
couple of bowls of chile, two tamales,
each hot and still in their cornhusks,
and returned. When he went down
into the cell-room, Farragut was too
hungry to swear at him.

They ate together, with the steel
bars between them, and from the
corridor Jim innocently said, "Leland,
were you figuring on having house-
guests?"

Farragut slowly raised a wrinkled
brow and sulphurous eyes. "What the
hell are you up to now, Blevins?
Where'm I going to put house-guests
in this lousy cell?"

"I didn't mean here, I meant at the
house. Maybe some kinfolk or some
old friends were about to visit."

"No dammit all, Blevins. What's
wrong with you anyway? Only kin I
got are so far off they'd be six months
even reaching the Territory. What the

hell's wrong with you anyway—you been drinking?"

Blevins nodded. "Yeah, a little."

It was the truth but one glass of beer had not had any effect upon Jim Blevins since he'd passed his sixteenth birthday. "Good tamales," he said amiably.

Instead of replying, Leland looked out and did exactly what those other two had done; looked with annoyed bafflement at the sheriff and shook his head.

In the roadway a freight outfit grinding up-country from Mexico nearly filled the full width and some cowboys arriving at the same time had to yield the right of way or get tangled up with a hitch of eight orry-eyed Mexican mules, so they swore at the grinning Mexican driver, who swore back at them grinning from ear to ear and since no one had the slightest idea what the others had said, everyone was satisfied, the cowboys rode around behind the big rig and the Mex mules pulled their burden all the way up out of town in the direction of a freighter-camp on the outskirts.

5

VISITORS

Blevins returned the empty bowls to the Mex cafe, encountered a man named Jess Hobbs over there who drove for the Territorial Stage & Cartage Company, and listened to a rambling dissertation about a six-foot rattler which had spooked his hitch north of Muletown and Hobbs had had all he'd been able to do to keep the coach right side up as the four horses took off in runaway-panic across the westerly desert. When it was all over, according to Jess Hobbs, a drummer whose sample cases had nearly beaten the other passengers back and blue, climbed down, walked out a ways and was sick to his stomach.

Hobbs shook his head. "And you know something, Sheriff; that feller didn't even see it was a rattlesnake. Just thought it was a normal runaway."

Tactful Jim Blevins murmured astonishment, which he was supposed to murmur, and got out of there.

In the roadway it occurred to him that the beer he'd had earlier had tasted almighty fine, so he went back to the saloon, got two buckets of suds and went back to the jailhouse.

He gave one bucket to Farragut and the prisoner peered out suspiciously. "If you figure one bucket of beer is goin' to make me say something I hadn't ought to say, you're in for a disappointment, Jim."

"Why do you always figure the worst about people," asked Blevins plaintively, and pulled up one of the little visitor's stools to sit upon out in the dingy corridor. "Just drink the beer. It's a nice evening and beer goes well with a nice evening."

Farragut drank, still looked sceptical, drank some more and began to loosen a little, so he went and sat upon the wall-bunk, which was the only place to sit, or lie, in his cell. "I'm obliged," he said, and added another sentence to it. "I never had a darned thing against you, Jim."

Blevins smiled. "Until you got to drinkin' too much, lately Leland, I felt the same way. As for this—I can't figure what you were expecting to do. We don't have bullion coaches down here but once in a blue moon, and not even very many passengers—specially this time of year. It was a foolish thing to do. If you'd had in mind robbing a coach you should have gone over by Albuquerque where they got a fort and a military payroll. Something like that."

"I didn't expect to get rich, I just

figured to get maybe a hundred dollars," grumbled Farragut, drinking more beer.

Jim scowled. "We don't have hundred-dollar stagecoaches down here. You ought to know that."

"Fifty then. Deuce needed some things. She's entitled to 'em."

Blevins wanly nodded. "That story again. Lee, I can think of a dozen good females right here in town that don't even have as much as Deuce has, and no one goes out to rob stages to make things better for them."

"Then their husbands aren't much!"

"Their husbands," replied Sheriff Blevins, "aren't in jail, Lee. And I don't expect any of those women would accept anything bought for them with stolen money."

"Jim, you should have been a preacher." As Farragut leaned to shove the empty suds bucket under the steel door, he loosed a rich, moist belch and straightened back with

obvious satisfaction. "It was good
beer, and by golly it sure was welcome. I'm right obliged to you, Jim."

Blevins swished his bucket and
watched the dregs form where he had
the bucket tipped. Then he threw back
his head, raised the bucket and swal-
lowed deeply. It was indeed good beer.
Lowering the container he offered an
observation. "Beer is the best thing a
man can drink with tamales and chili.
I always wondered why Mexes drank
wine instead."

"They don't drink beer very much,
and anyway that *cerbeza* they
make ..." Farragut made an exag-
gerated shudder.

"And a smoke," said Blevins, as
though Farragut had not spoken. "A
man needs a smoke to go with his
cerbeza and tamales." He suddenly
snapped his fingers. "I forgot; I was
going to fetch you some tobacco."

Farragut held up his limp bag of
tobacco and Blevins dug around for a

fuller one and pitched it towards the bunk through the bars. "Until I get a full one at the store," he explained. "Anyway, I don't smoke very much. I sort of quit. Like Deuce, I'm getting away from the habit."

Farragut turned. "Deuce don't smoke. She never did, that I know of."

Blevins's brow puckered. "I thought ... Maybe it was someone else."

"Must've been, Jim, because my wife don't never use tobacco. Good thing too. I don't like womenfolk to smell of stale tobacco. Do you?"

Blevins had smelled neither tobacco nor French toilet water, nor even clean sage-scent on a woman since his wife had died, but he agreed. "Nope, I sure don't." Then he arose, kicked away the stool and leaned to retrieve the second empty beer pail. "Someone told Arnie Ferguson there is a circuit rider on his way, Lee. Maybe you'd like that because now you'll get this waiting over with one way or another."

Farragut did not comment, he was lighting a cigarette.

Blevins returned to his office, locked the steel-belted oak door at his back, went thoughtfully back across to get rid of the beer pails, nodded when some townsmen greeted him, and came all the way back to his office wrapped in deep thought.

Later, with shadows puddling along the roadway edges, he went up to the stage office and asked about incoming coaches. The yardboss up there gave him a hand-written schedule, scratched under the green eyeshade, resettled the thing and cast a wondering look at Blevins.

"This is the first time you taken that much interest, Jim. Don't tell me Farragut got out."

Blevins was reading the schedule in weak daylight as he replied. "Naw; he's still locked up. I was just curious is all. Tell me, Hugh, any money or big sacks of mail or bullion—anything valuable coming in on any of these stages?"

The man with the eyeshade looked pained. "Coming to Muletown?"

Blevins nodded. "That's what I figured," he said, and turned to depart. He halted in the late-day shadows of the doorway and turned. "What you got on schedule up from Sonora, over the line?"

Hugh went to a littered desk and leaned a moment, frowning. Then he said, "Freight for Arnie, mostly oranges and stuff like that, and a couple crates of Mex cotton." He looked up. "Why?"

It was a good question. Why— would anyone have any interest in stages which did not have anything of value on them coming from the north to Muletown, and why would anyone be interested in Sonora oranges and

Mex cotton coming up from the south?

They wouldn't have, Blevins told himself as he left the stage office on his way down to within a short distance of the liverybarn.

Maybe, what he had figured out, wasn't making any sense after all. On the other hand, what made even less sense was Deuce buying enough food to feed a cavalry squadron, *and* tobacco which she did not use, and which she had not asked Blevins if she could take to her husband.

The riddle had its answer at the cottage out behind Farragut's shoeing-shed, but when he got down there the place was closed up and locked, Deuce was not at home.

The disappointment was less than the increased interest this occasioned. Blevins went out back. The grulla horse and one of the saddles was also gone. Well; that pretty well took care of the questions he had wanted to ask. For the time being at any rate.

He returned to the jailhouse beginning to believe that Deuce had not only deliberately shot Buff so that her husband would have to surrender, or perhaps even get killed while she hid, but also because she had some other scheme in mind in which she did not want her husband involved.

A lot of groceries and tobacco told Jim Blevins that whatever this scheme was, it involved men, and Blevins was willing to wager money on that.

He cudgelled his brain for something; anything at all either Leland or his wife might have said to offer a clue and came up with nothing at all, so he arose and drank from the *olla*, wiped his chin and when John Colendar walked in, Blevins nodded without much enthusiasm and returned to the chair behind his table, under the quizzical glance and hoisted dark eyebrows of his friend.

Colendar took a chair, shoved out his legs, pressed thumb-pads together and said, "You are stumped. Well, it's happened to all of us and the world hasn't stopped rolling over and over."

Blevins stared without smiling. If John Colendar had any serious faults one of them had to be his patronising way of talking. He probably did not mean to sound that way, probably had never meant to act like that although in his line of work, dealing with people every day who knew less of his speciality than he knew, it probably was easy for men like John to slip into an almost unconscious response based upon superiority.

Blevins said, "There is just one thing that stumps me, John. How Lee Farragut could have lived with Deuce as long as he has, and never even guessed she's known other men now and then since they've been married. And that makes me wonder—what other men are still coming around?"

Colendar still sat with thumbs pressing together. "One time over at Springville I saw her with a tall feller who wore an ivory-stocked sixshooter and had droopy whiskers like a dragoon officer. I stepped into a store and let them march past. Not much point in embarrassing hell out of both of us."

Blevins reared back in the chair. He could recall seeing Deuce with at least a dozen men over the past few years. It had been a source of wonder to him that Leland had never found out. She had to indeed be a very clever woman.

Now, within the past week, he'd had occasion to surmise just *how* clever, and of course this was what was troubling him now.

"What is it?" asked the doctor. "She hasn't been to see Leland?"

Blevins almost snorted out loud. He waited a moment, then said, "She never had any intention of coming to see him."

Colendar had no difficulty believing

that. "Then what is it that's got you upset?"

"What she's up to now," stated Blevins, speaking against his better judgement, at least speaking out in a manner he had learned long ago not to do, as a peace officer, except that in this instance he knew his man.

"Just because she rode out of town this morning?"

Blevins pounced on that. "You saw her?"

"Sure; right up the alley out back when I was out there dumping trash. Riding that sort of odd-coloured bluish horse I've seen her ride the last year or so. Heading north." Doc settled both hands in his lap for a change. "The time? Oh, I'd guess it was about eight o'clock. Pretty early but then I figured that perhaps she was going on a long ride."

If she had been gone that long—all day—there was no chance of Blevins overtaking her, and now that evening was approaching there was no way for him to track her very far either.

"Have saddlebags or a pack, John?"

Doctor Colendar had to pause and think back. He had not been very interested at eight o'clock that morning, in a long-legged big-breasted woman, a delightful sunrise, or much of anything else.

"Saddlebags as I recollect," he affirmed. "Pretty well pouched out at that. Full of something."

Blevins said, "Yeah. Full of tinned peaches and beef and tobacco and other stuff." He leaned forward. "I'll be damned."

Colendar gravely nodded. "That sure is a good possibility," he said and arose. "What I came down here to tell you was that I'll be sending Buff Rhodes back to the ranch in the morning. I sent word out for them to come get him in a wagon. Had no idea whether you care or not, Jim, but thought I'd tell you."

Blevins did not care. He arose to go to the door with John Colendar and had scarcely seen his friend out when that west-country cowman Harry Horton, one of the possemen when they'd captured Leland Farragut, tied up out front and came in spanking off dust with his sweat-stained, greasy and disreputable old hat.

Horton bobbed his head, went to the *olla*, drank deeply, threw out a big sigh and took the chair the doctor had relinquished as he said, "Been cuttin' back Mex cattle for two days. Some Messican down yonder was drivin' west towards *Baja*, a lightning storm hit right over him, and he said he's got cattle scattered from back to Chihuahua forward towards the California line. Me, so far I've cut back sixty-six head ... Hard work, Sheriff. Not like settin' in that chair all day long."

Blevins's temper stirred but he controlled it without effort. "Too bad your daddy forced you into the cattle business, Harry."

Horton fished for the makings as though he had not been rebuffed. "That Messican told me some *gringos* busted into a rich *ranchero's* place down there in Sonora, shot three people and cleaned out the old gentleman's safe and moneybox, then lit out on the best thoroughbreds the *hacendado* had in his stable." Horton smiled. "Sure nice to have our men hitting them for a change."

Blevins shifted in the chair. "Been curious. Haven't heard a thing since we run down Lee Farragut and brought him in. Didn't escape did he?"

That also made Jim's blood pressure go up a notch. He had never lost a prisoner out of the Muletown jailhouse. "He didn't escape, Harry, and you want to be sure to give that Mex back all his critters, even the ones get tucked up in some sagebrush canyon."

Horton's eyes widened. "What in hell kind of a thing is that to say?"

Blevins answered tartly. "Same kind you've been putting out ever since you walked in here."

Horton continued to stare a moment longer then arose and went to the door where, one hand on the latch, he turned and said, "You got cabin-fever, Sheriff. You'd ought to get out in the fresh air for a few days." He walked out and closed the door after himself.

Blevins called Horton a bad name and stood up reaching for his hat. Unless Deuce Farragut did not intend to return today she would probably be getting back to town shortly.

He went outside, saw Harry over across in front of the general store talking and wagging his head while Arnold Ferguson was listening. Blevins did not need second-sight or whatever it was to guess what Horton was telling the storekeeper—about Blevins.

He walked southward and the settling night was all around, pleasantly warm and moonless but with pale stars up there by the corralful, and far out somewhere east of town, east even of Mex town which lay upon the far side of *gringo*-town, a desert fox yapped repeatedly for about a full half minute. They did that to tease town dogs, and it worked this time as it almost invariably did. Dogs from both parts of town sat back and howled back.

6

"POR NADA"

Deuce was not down there, but as Blevins stood in the gloom speculating on how far she must have ridden not to have returned yet, after leaving at eight o'clock this morning, he detected the steady hoof-fall sound of a tired horse coming down the back alley from up north.

He moved over to the shed, looked around, decided waiting inside might be better since there was no decent cover outside, and explored the stygian darkness in the shed until he found a narrow place between the wall and the stack of meadow hay where he could fit.

There was no particular plan. In

fact when he'd first arrived down here he'd had in mind asking questions, and right up until he had stepped into the shed that had still been his idea, but now as he pressed in flat and waited where the darkness was deepest, another idea crossed his mind.

Deuce dismounted in the alley and led her horse on through into the dark yard, growled for the grulla to be quiet and after looking around, turned to get closer, where a stud-ring embedded in a tree served as her tie-rack.

Blevins could not see her but he heard her grunt as she lifted down the saddle, heard her dragging bootsteps as she came over into the shed and grunted a second time as she heaved the outfit across its saddlepole. Then she returned to the yard for the horse. She was dog-tired and Blevins did not have to be able to see her to realise that. She was walking like a person who did not have a single spring left in their ankles.

The grulla was no better off. Even after she stalled him and pitched in hay, he simply stood there head-hung. She said, "Tough son of a bitch wasn't it?"and left the shed on her way to the back of the house.

Blevins made a little clucking sound of dismay over her candid comment, then eased out, waited until the light shone from the house, and went over to lift off the sweaty saddleblanket and grope in darkness for the buckles of her saddlebags.

The bags were empty except for an embroidered scarf which someone had painstakingly worked on for weeks, perhaps even months. It was a magnificent thing, silk but stiffened by the three-dimensional bulge of love-birds cheek to cheek upon a treelimb against a brilliant background of leaves and flowers.

Blevins took it out back where the starlight helped him examine it. He shook his head and pocketed the shawl. Deuce Farragut would look about as appropriate in that prayer-shawl as Blevins would look in one of Deuce's brassie ... *prayer-shawl*!

He stepped into the back alley and unfurled the thing for a closer examination. It was indeed a shawl of the kind devout Mexican women covered their heads with while inside a church, except that this one had not belonged to just any Mexican woman, this one had cost someone a lot of money and had without question belonged to a lady.

The *hacendada*! The wife sure as hell of the raided *hacendado* down in Sonora!

Blevins leaned on the old fence gazing steadily at the light in the blacksmith's house across the weed-grown unkempt back lot. After a long time he turned and walked slowly up the alley to the first dog-trot, crossed through to emerge upon the Main Street duckboards and turned southward again, this time making his approach in the normal manner, so normal in fact that as he turned in at the neglected gate he rattled the thing and otherwise made noise on his way to the porch.

Deuce opened the door and looked at her caller, heavy hair cut short and gleaming in poor lamplight from behind, her riding clothes shed so that she could stand as she did now in a loose-fitting Mexican dress which, loose-fitting or not, could not be *that* loose-fitting without falling off, so she was facing Blevins as a very striking big-busted woman, unsmiling and quizzical.

Blevins removed his hat. "Wondered if you'd thought any more about selling the grulla horse."

She hesitated without removing her glance from Blevins's face. Then finally she said, "Really, Sheriff, is that why you came down here tonight?"

He almost smiled. "No. Wanted to ask you some questions."

Now, Deuce sagged against the doorjamb in a clear expression of tired wonder. "Tonight? I'm tired, Sheriff."

"Yeah. You went horseback riding. I been down here before today and the horse was gone."

"And what of it?"

He said, "Nothing. I just figured if you had a few minutes this evening ..."

She did not step aside for him to enter, she instead pushed on outside to the little dark porch and closed the door behind herself. "Have a chair," she said tonelessly, and moved to take another one nearby. As she sank down she looked a little coquettishly upwards. "If you don't let my husband out pretty soon, Sheriff, I'm going to get awful lonesome."

He shoved back his hat after seating himself. "Anyone as good-looking as you won't ever be lonesome for long, Deuce."

Her heavy lips parted. "Why Sheriff Blevins!"

He ignored that. "You were in the rocks with Leland when he tried to rob the stage north of town, Deuce."

It was too dark between them for him to be able to catch a change in her face, nor was she a woman who could be jarred into blurting out anything, not even a fierce denial. She waited, then said, "Who told you that?"

It would have been very easy to lie, to tell her Leland had told him, but he knew what the reaction on her part would be to any such statement. She would denounce it, and her husband, and maybe jump up and go into the house.

He told her the truth in a mild tone of voice. "I went back up there. Found your tracks and the place where you'd tied the grulla horse."

She sounded sceptical as she said,

"Did you *see* me; did anyone else *see* me up there? Then you just go ahead and believe what you want to believe, Sheriff Blevins!"

He could of course have mentioned her Lightning Colt and the bullet taken from Buff Rhodes. In fact he could have arrested her on the strength of what he had in the way of circumstantial evidence, but if he brought her to trial on what he had, any circuit judge worth his salt would throw the case out.

He said, "You set that darned fool up like a tenpin for me to knock over, Deuce, and I came right along and did it as you wanted me to."

She relaxed back into her chair watching his shadowy profile. "Sheriff," she said in a quieter voice, "we've been enemies since our trails first crossed."

"There's been reason," he murmured, then swung a little so that he was facing her.

She brushed that aside with impatience. "Hell, if you want to dislike someone you don't never have to hunt far to find a reason. All right; I can guess what your reason has been ... Sheriff; they tell me you're not a drinking man."

"Not a very *good* one, anyway."

"Will you come inside and have a drink with me?" she asked without taking her bold eyes off his face.

He audibly sighed. She was certainly a handsome woman. He got to his feet looking down at her. "Ten years ago, Deuce, I'd have been the first one to do that with you. Now just answer one more question for me and I'll leave you alone. Where did you ride today?"

She came up out of her chair in one supple movement. "It's none of your damned business!" she exclaimed and hastened past and slammed the door after herself.

He smiled a trifle bitterly and

meandered back to the plankwalk heading north, but two-thirds of the way along he crossed to the far side of the road and set a steady course for the saloon. Not for another beer, this time, but to see if Harry Horton were still in town.

Harry was. They had him boxed in at a poker session and when Sheriff Blevins leaned to murmur that he needed to talk, Horton had the excuse he needed to cash in and get out. The other players fixed Blevins with looks ranging from frank hostility to icy disapproval. He smiled and walked towards the lower end of the bar with Horton. He flagged for two jolts, then he leaned a trifle sideways and said, "The Mexes who told you about gringo *raiders attacking some ranch down south—are they still at your camp?*"

"Was when I left this morning. As far as I know they figure to stay until we finish splitting out their critters. Another day maybe. What of it?"

"Well; when they told you of that attack down yonder, they didn't by any chance say they knew this rancher, or his ranch, or anything like that, did they?"

Horton thought back as he started to wag his head. "They didn't mention that at all, Jim. Didn't say anything more than what I told you." Horton saw the drinks arrive, watched the sheriff count out the exact coinage and put it atop the bar, then lift his drink and turn back to say, "How many raiders was there, Harry?"

Horton also reached for a glass. "If they told me I didn't catch it. I'm sorry. But if it's real important you could ride back with me tonight ... What's this all about, anyway?"

Blevins downed his drink and said, "You ready to ride?" He did not offer a reply to Horton's question and as they made their way out into the cooling night heading south for their horses, Horton did not seem to remember that his question still hung between them.

It was a cool night, finally, and it was getting steadily cooler as they rode overland in an easy lope. Not much was said. Blevins was busy with his private thoughts, and evidently the cowman also was. Once, where they went slightly out of their way because Horton wanted to check a salt-log, they paused long enough for Horton to say, "By golly they *did* say how many of them raiders there was, Jim. They said three. I just now recalled that."

Four miles farther along they came upon a big clearing in the desert where a cow-camp had been established years before. There was not a building of any kind out there, but someone had spent a lot of time and effort creating a series of faggot-corrals, high enough and dense enough to discourage the kind of jumping cattle they had down on the south desert.

Otherwise it looked pretty much like every other cow-camp, except that down here the *texas* which offered shade during midday was strung between huge thornpin bushes and permitted about ten men to get beneath it at one time even though Harry Horton had never employed more than five riders at any time.

The place was quiet but there was still a pungent scent of chili on the air which indicated that the *vaqueros* had not rolled in very long ago.

There were two wagons, one with bows and a canvas top. Some men slept inside and some slept beneath those vehicles.

The Mexicans, though, were slightly apart and had their more colourful robes and blankets arranged so that if anyone came walking over in the darkness, or if some horses got loose from the remuda, they would not be caught unprepared. Harry took Blevins over there, stopped to point at the ground where a thin length of rawhide had been stretched between sticks and grimaced. "They always figure we're going to sneak up on 'em at night and slit their throats" he dropped his arm. "By daytime they're just like anyone else."

Blevins did not need the lecture. He stepped over the boot-trap, knelt next to a large inert bundle beneath a multicoloured serape, figured which hand the Mexican probably had either a gun or knife in, and when he leaned to gently awaken the man he was poised to pin him.

But the Mexican raised up looking from Horton, whom he recognised, to the man wearing the badge whom he had never seen before. In abominable Spanish, Horton said, "He wants to ask you of those attack by which you told me—down in Sonora."

The *vaquero* was large, heavy, very

dark and pock-marked. If he had been in a priest's robes he still would have looked villainous.

His name was Duran. Emilio Duran, he told Blevins, and stifled a yawn then vigorously scratched under the serape. He knew so little English it was fortunate Blevins spoke fluent— but not necessarily grammatical— Spanish.

When Blevins asked specific questions, Emilio Duran, with the cobwebs cleared from his head, answered quickly. He did indeed know the *rancho* which had been raided. In fact of the three *vaqueros* who had been shot and killed as the raiders charged in, one had been the son of his wife's aunt's adopted sister, a woman named Estralita Veira.

Blevins resigned himself to it; he had one of those Mexicans who endlessly elaborated. A lot of them were like that. But when Blevins fished forth the shawl, shook it out and held it in the starlight for Emilio Duran to see, the silence drew out so long Blevins thought Duran had lost his voice.

In a way he had. When the words finally came, all in a rush, it turned out that his wife's aunt had herself created that prayer-shawl for the mistress of the raided ranch, the devout and very beautiful *Senora* Paz de la Gutierrez-Guzman y Montoya-Diaz. Duran looked at Blevins, then at Harry Horton, then back to Blevins. "You found this where?" he enquired. "*Senor,* when I get back and explain to the *ranchero* who you are and that you have this thing, he will come and see you."

It sounded more to Blevins like a threat than anything else. As he pocketed the scarf he said, "It was given to a lady, friend, and what I seek to discover is who this man is to give the thing to her. You understand?"

Duran nodded his head. He was

now wide awake and around him in the darkness other dark heads were up and listening, but no Mexican made a sound, nor, more distantly over near those old wagons, did any of the *americanos* make a sound. Their reason for not doing so was more legitimate; they were without exception sound asleep.

Blevins arose and looked from Horton to the hanging big graniteware coffee pot at the stone ring where the camp meals were prepared. His last word to Emilio Duran was a simple question: "Do you know any other thing about those three bandits?"

Duran did not. "Only that they came just before dawn, shot three sentries at the *rancho*, and stole everything of value from inside, then got away on stolen horses even before the sun could arise."

"*Gracias.*"

Duran nodded his head. "*Por nada, jefe.*"

Over at the fire Harry Horton tipped the pot to draw off two cupfuls of incredibly black and oily-looking coffee. When he handed over a cup he said, "What lady had that scarf?"

Blevins tasted the coffee and made a face. "How the hell can you drink that stuff?" he demanded, and put aside the cup. "I've got a long ride back. Harry, I'm obliged for your help."

They stood a moment gazing at each other then Horton said, "Yeah" in his dryest tone of voice.

7

THE LONG RIDE

When Blevins had been hiding in the Farragut horse-shed he'd thought of making a particular point of spying on Deuce. Now, as he loped eastward across the empty night, he made up his mind that it had to be more than that, he had to also go wherever she went.

Unless there was one hell of a mistake somewhere, and unless he'd ought to be ashamed of himself for thinking such terrible things about a woman, Deuce Farragut was in touch with those outlaws who had raided the *rancho* over the line in Sonora; had bought food and tobacco and had taken it out on the desert somewhere to them. One of them had given her the scarf. Her most glaring error was to forget the thing and leave it in the saddlebag instead of taking it with her into the house.

He tried to imagine if there was a connection between that, and the way she had set her husband up to be apprehended by the law. The best he could do on that question was to shake his head.

Deuce was a woman Blevins could not compare with any other woman he had ever met, and she was not the first female renegade he had run across.

The town was quiet when he rode in from the west and roused a sleeping nighthawk down at the liverybarn so his animal would be taken care of. The hostler looked completely surprised. Evidently no one had told him the sheriff had ridden out this evening. Maybe there was no reason why anyone should have told him, except that things like local lawmen, their comings and goings, were unfailingly a matter of concern in every cowtown west of the Missouri.

Blevins should have been tired. He was in fact cold, so he went to the office, got an old jacket, then went down the back alley to make certain the leg-worn grulla horse was still there. He was, full as a tick and sound asleep. Blevins did not waken him, but went soundlessly back out to the alley and returned to his office.

He did not light the lamp. He dug around behind the gun-case and emerged with a bottle of whisky. He mixed that with branch-water from the *olla*, took it to his desk, pitched aside the hat, hoisted spurred boots atop the table and leaned far back. He still was not tired. He usually did not get very tired when he had something like a riddle troubling him.

The whisky and water did a lot for him. A half-hour later he mixed another one and took it down into the cell-room, roused his sleeping prisoner and held the glass through the bars as Farragut rolled over, scowled, swung his feet to the floor and eyed the glass, then swore.

"Jim, you damned numbskull! What in the hell you think you're doing at this time of night, comin' round to shake a man out of a decent sleep?"

"Didn't know your conscience would allow you to sleep that deeply," replied Blevins. "Here, take this glass. It's just whisky and water. I just had one and it sure felt good. Take it."

Farragut did not budge from the edge of his bunk. "You're crazy. You think whisky's goin' to do what the pail of beer didn't do?"

"I am *not* trying to get you to talk," replied the lawman. "You want this or don't you? If you don't I'll take it back up yonder and drink it myself."

Farragut got stiffly to his feet and held out his hand for the glass. He went back to the bunk-edge and mightily yawned. "What time is it?"

Blevins, who did not carry a watch, made a rough guess—and it was 'rough'. "About midnight."

Farragut turned a sceptical face. "Midnight? Hell, they was hollering in the road a long while before I went to sleep that it was midnight." He drank some of the watered whisky. "How's come you to still be awake?"

"Been thinking, Leland."

Farragut shook his head. "Here come the darned questions." He drained the glass and shuddered. "That's mighty good whisky. Didn't come out of some horse-barn for a change."

"Came from Phoenix. Some freighters I used to work with a little when I first came out here, usually fetch along a bottle on their way through. Leland, there were three fellers in town asking about you today," lied Blevins. "Rough men, maybe rangeriders or horse-hunters."

Farragut thought before speaking.

"Can't place 'em. What was their names?"

Blevins felt like swearing. He had lost his gamble. He could tell from Farragut's face he was not being cute, that he had not slyly guessed what Blevins was doing—pumping him with questions interspersed through their normal conversation.

"I didn't here their names," Jim stated. "I think they went down to visit with Deuce."

Farragut really did not know any threesome. He clinched Jim's conviction about that when he said. "Could be fellers I've shod for, or maybe riders I used to go with years back ... Jim; you sure you went and told Deuce everything? How's it come she hasn't come to see me? Hey— damn you, Blevins!—did she try, and you turned her away?"

Jim could be absolutely honest about this. "If she'd come up here I'd have let her see you. If she comes tomorrow it's fine with me, I'm not going to stop her."

Blevins was getting nowhere and now he began to feel sleepy so as he straightened up off the bar he shoved through a thick arm. "Give me the empty glass and go on back to sleep."

Farragut handed over the glass, stepped to his side of the barred door and watched Blevins retreat up in the direction of his office. This was the second time that Leland Farragut could not understand something Sheriff Blevins had done.

It did not trouble him for long. He lay back on the cot again, snored within five minutes and this time made it all the way through to dawnlight without an interruption. When he awakened his mouth tasted like the Mex army had marched across it barefoot and the last *mestizo* had scraped his feet.

He was not alone. When Blevins rolled out he felt about the same way.

Maybe that was indeed good whisky, but it sure would have left them both feeling better if they had eaten something before downing it.

Blevins went out back in the alley to the washrack and propped up his mirror to shave. He went through the entire ritual before turning to look southward, down in the direction of the liverybarn where the dayman who had just come to work was leading out pairs of haltered horses to be turned into the daytime corrals.

There was an ajar gate down there. It hit Blevins like a blow in the chest because last night he had been the final person to pass out into the alley from the gateway and he had made sure out of long habit to see that the thing was latched. He remembered latching it.

He flung away the wash water, grabbed his soap and razor and towel and ran back inside to grab his shirt, button it one-handedly while he grabbed for his shellbelt with the other hand.

Farragut was going to miss breakfast. As a matter of fact he was more and more the victim and less and less the criminal in all this.

Blevins went speedily to the liverybarn, hurried on through into the back-alley where the hostler was dunging out, and asked if the dayman had seen Mrs Farragut ride out. The dayman leaned upon his manure-fork with a dreamy expression upon his face as he replied.

"You know, if a man had a woman like that, Sheriff, life'd be just almost worth puttin' up with."

"If you had that one, *amigo*, you'd think life was worth puttin' up with all right. Did you see her ride out?"

"Yeah." The hostler raised an arm to point westward, then dropped the arm and sighed again. "She's put up like a lady woodtick and that's a pure fact."

"How long ago did she ride out?"

The hostler was languid about answering. He also seemed too preoccupied to be entirely accurate. "Well; seems like it was maybe an hour ago. Naw, it warn't that long, Sheriff Blevins. More like fifteen minutes ago." The hostler suddenly remembered something. "That blue horse of hers warn't right up in the bit this morning, maybe he's got a touch of the epizootic. We get it around here almost every Monday morning."

Blevins did not order the man to go get his own horse. It was worth it to get away from that insipid individual and do it himself.

He was going to miss breakfast too. Not that it bothered him very much; when his mind was fully occupied he could go for long periods of time without eating and it did not appear to bother him.

The hostler had evidently recovered from his rapturous reflections about

Deuce Farragut, and in fact as Blevins rode out and saw the man swinging his laden manure-fork with sturdy ability it occurred to him that perhaps there were few jobs on earth which could dampen rapturous ardour as thoroughly as cleaning out a liverybarn in the morning.

He had no idea what was ahead, whether Deuce had not changed course or even that she was not watching him boot out his animal in obvious pursuit, but he *did* know one thing, he nor anyone else could have tracked her because all the territory around Muletown for several miles had hundreds of shod-horse marks; one of the curses of being in an area where it never rained in summertime.

Blevins had never been an individual who entertained many illusions. Without being certain of it he was satisfied that Deuce knew the desert. It happened that he also knew it; had an idea that he probably knew it better than she did.

It was in fact this conviction plus one other, that made Blevins seek at least a sighting on ahead so that he could know in which direction she was riding.

It was that 'one other' conviction which kept him believing he would not have to actually keep her in sight to find out where she was going. The south desert was notorious for two things—heat and lack of water. The heat was waning at this autumn time of year. As for the water, *that* was the clue; wherever she was heading to complete what he felt certain was a rendezvous, there had to be water. Those renegades could not camp for long without it.

There were some springs, but not very many. In fact there were very few still running this late in the season. Blevins knew them all, and the ones west of Muletown were spread out

over a vast area. In order to correctly surmise which spring she was heading for he had to know which direction she was riding in. After that, he would not need to follow her, he could choose his own route towards the waterhole.

But the curse of the south desert in this respect was that it was flat. Elsewhere all a person had to do was ride up atop a knoll. Down here the land lay flat for hundreds of brushy miles. Not only flat but for much of the distance there were stands of thicket, thornpin, wiry sage, and a whole host of other varieties which grew about as tall as a mounted man hindering visibility. Only the indigenous Apaches had learned over the millennia how to turn this to a distinct advantage. The annals of Southwestern history were full of ambushes where Apaches lying at the base of flourishing big brush-stands, had caught on-coming enemies unawares, and had massacred them.

Blevins knew little of Apaches but he knew something about manhunting in this environment because he'd had plenty of occasions since arriving out here to do it.

By jogging westward from town for two miles he had at least lessened the distance between them, and after that when he sank back to a steady walk he rode standing in the stirrups. In places where it was possible to see over the top of the undergrowth, he had an opportunity to catch flashes of onward countryside. In places where even standing did not help, he started sashaying back and forth looking for horse-sign.

Once, he found an encouraging fresh set of dug-in tracks indicating that someone had very recently booted out their horse. The sand was still crumbling from the hoof-ridges, in fact, and was sifting down into the impression left by the horse's frog. If it was not Deuce then it had to be someone just as anxious to be elsewhere. Nor was that impossible; the south desert had wraiths crossing it in a hurry to drop below the line before the law caught up with them, by day as well as by night.

He grew cautious after finding those tracks, and although he followed them for a short while, they swung abruptly southward and held to that fresh course with unerring determination, so he turned northward again, because there was no water in the direction that rider was taking until he got over the line to the Mexican village of Duarte, which had to be his destination. People did not just accidentally go arrow-straight to the border, which was not marked except by little cairns of small white-painted stones, unless they either knew, or had a map to show them, how to get down there.

He struck back northward following

an onward angling route. And this time he made a contact.

In the morning hush a horse coughed! It could have been a half-mile distant but the *direction* could not be that distorted. The rider was angling northward from where Blevins had last been riding before he scouted out those other fresh tracks.

Northward about six miles was a sump-spring and a roofless ancient goatherder's humble adobe one-room house—a *jacal.*

Blevins halted, swung to the ground, and Indian-like, squatted with desert-bred patience. It was a long wait and when the second sound arrived in that crystal clear air, it was not another cough it was the shuffling small drag of tired shod hooves over pebbles.

Blevins knew only one horse tired enough to be dragging this early in the day. He smiled mirthlessly and fixed the course of the invisible rider in his mind, then arose to go walking ahead leading his horse, following in his mind's eye the route of the person up ahead.

There were clearings, and once, Blevins caught the scent of nearby cattle but he did not see them. From here on flies followed along bothering his horse, so there had indeed been cattle back there. Wild or not, one thing cattle learned quickly in desert country was to emulate the wildlife; to stand utterly motionless when someone went by. Nine times out of ten it worked—but the cattlemen had their own answer to that; dogs.

His horse picked up the scent, of course, but cattle were no novelty to the horse while whatever the man leading him on ahead was up to certainly was a novelty. The horse, strongly curious, followed and watched and listened.

It was in fact the horse which finally warned Blevins. He hung back a fraction, and just as Blevins turned the horse raised his head to nicker.

Blevins yanked the reins, then caught hold of the horse's nostrils pinching off the air for a moment. It worked; the horse did not make a sound.

Blevins shook his head at the animal, gradually eased up on the nostrils, and by he time he was ready to continue his walk into the northward underbrush the horse was over his urge to announce their presence.

8

DISCOVERY!

Because by nature Blevins was one of those individuals who, even when satisfied about something, required additional verification, he finally left the horse far back, tethered to a paloverde, and jogged ahead for a full mile to be thoroughly convinced that he was not following another of those wraiths.

The reward was fleeting. When he finally detected the rump of a grulla horse its rider was twisted, looking rearward. Blevins stepped into a thicket and turned to stone. If she was simply being cautious, fine, if she had somehow surmised he was back there ...

She straightened forward, stood in

the stirrups to peer far ahead, and Blevins finally could breathe normally again. She had simply been observing predictable caution, but what was more to the point he had seen her. Not just the horse but Deuce as well.

He did not hasten back and when he finally was in the saddle again, he reined off eastward and pushed over into an easy lope. He knew exactly where he was going, he knew exactly how to get up there, and he was pretty well convinced what he would find when he got up there.

The heat came, but nowhere nearly as bad as it would have been two months earlier. The underbrush had dust on it, the ground underfoot shaded from sandy loam to cracked and brittle adobe. There were snakes and lizards, even a couple of inert, fat old gila monsters on his route, and once he picked up that cow-scent again, but this time because he was getting close to Harry Horton's turnout he was not at all surprised. Again, though, he did not see the critters.

Those far-distant smoky old mountains were blue-blurred and barren looking from this far off. They were actually a kind of borderland between the south desert and the cooler, more timbered grassland territory northward a hundred or so miles.

Blevins had an idea the renegades up ahead would be heading overland towards those mountains. He speculated about Deuce; would she be trailing along with them?

He winced at the thought of Leland, back there in his jail cell absolutely innocent of any knowledge of this thing his wife was embroiled in.

There was an adage: 'Blacksmith stick to your anvil'. It had never been more accurately applied than right now to Lee Farragut.

To kill time as he rode, Blevins went over in great detail all he remembered of the onward area up around that goatherder's spring, and by the time he was as close as he thought it prudent to get, he had worked out a fairly good system for approaching without being seen.

He widened the distance until there occurred an oat-grass clearing, evidently fed by the same distant underground vein of water which fed the sump-spring over at the goatherder's clearing, and here he found a stunted tree of nondescript origin standing alone amid the oat-grass. If Horton's cattle knew of this place they certainly had not returned to it because the grass was almost five feet tall and heading out. In another few days it would be in the dough. No cow Blevins had ever known would not have walked a long distance to find oat-grass at this stage of its annual development.

His horse welcomed the discovery too, but Blevins only allowed him to browse very briefly before tying him short in tree-shade, lifting out his Winchester from the saddleboot, and turning to cross into the dusty brush as he struck out on foot.

From here, he estimated that he had about two miles to cover, and fortunately along with his inherent sense of direction, the sun was bright but there was very little actual heat. At least it was not hot on the desert in the ways that Blevins knew it could be and for most of the year, usually was.

He covered the first mile handily, then changed course often, obscuring tracks whenever he could, utilised every bit of cover, waited for long periods in still and quiet shade, studied the ground often, and in the end got northward of the sump-spring clearing because he believed neither Deuce nor her friends would be up in that area, and he was correct. There were no signs up there to even indicate that the raiders had explored north of the spring.

It was the smell of cooking which alerted him, first, and a little later as he crept from bush to bush, from shade-patch to bush again, he could pick up voices. But he was not as close as this might have indicated. Sound on the south desert but especially this time of year when the air was completely clear, carried almost endlessly.

He paused to pull loose the sixgun-tiedown, to stand a while listening, then he started forward and saw movement dead ahead through the limbs of an old chaparral bush which was at least ten feet tall.

Three horses were hobbled and browsing upon the far side of the big bush. He dropped low, pushed deeper into the thorny old unfriendly bush, waited until he had seen the left shoulder of each animal, and had another patch of evidence to add to the other little indications. *Those horses wore Mexican brands!*

Unless Destiny was playing one hell

of a trick on Jim Blevins; those horses turned out to belong to simply three *vaqueros*; he was getting very close to something he wanted to know a whole of a lot more about.

To avoid arousing the animals he had to shift course, to go farther west. It required a little time. There were more clearings over there, evidently hand-made by some long-gone Mexican goatherder whose little world of harmless pleasures had been abruptly ended by an Apache bullet, and no one now even remembered his name.

The clearings were godsends to all the local wildlife, but they were not favourable to Jim Blevins. He had to go twice as far out and around before he dared trying angling in towards the sump-spring area again.

The voices tapered off for a while, the smell of cooking grew stronger, and when Blevins knew he was close was when a man's words clearly carried.

"No need to hurry. Messican *rurales* dassn't cross over the line any more'n U.S. lawmen can go down there on a chase, and by the time they work something out—see them damned mountains? We'll be so far north of them won't nobody ever find us."

Blevins crept into a big bush, got belly-down and eased gingerly forward until he saw a man lean and pitch dry chaparral onto a little fire.

The camp was unkempt with horse-gear scattered, with booted carbines slanted here and there indiscriminately, and with several Mexican *alforjas*—pack boxes, or panniers— standing together. Each *alforja* had the same spidery brand burned into the rawhide as had also been burned into the living flesh of those three hobbled horses.

Blevins, who had ceased to require additional conviction some time back, eyed the *alforjas* wondering which of

them the beautiful little prayer-shawl
had come from.

A large whiskered individual, broad
and thick but not really very old,
perhaps in his mid-twenties, came out
of the shade to stand with his oaken
legs wide-sprung while he filled a tin
cup with coffee and said, "Arch; I'll
give you back them gold Mex
doubleagles you lost last night, for
that big silver crucifix."

The leaning man who had fed the
fire grumbled a surly answer. "I'll get
even. I'll get my stuff back and more
when we start up the poker game
tonight."

The big man laughed. "You just
don't never win at poker. By now
you'd ought to know that." The big
man's easy, good-natured voice carried
out a little ways. "Deuce; you ever
know a feller who never won at poker
before?"

Blevins tried to see around those big

oaken legs and failed. But he knew the voice.

"Yeah, I sure do know one. He never won at just about anything else, either ... Toke?"

The big man answered in what seemed to Blevins to be his standard tone of voice; patronisingly. "You worryin' again, Deuce? Forget it. Come nightfall and we'll be gettin' farther and farther."

She said, "Why wait? That's what I was going to say. Out here there is only one cow-outfit, and that's east of us a ways. Outside of that you've got clear sailing all the way into the mountains. But it worries me—waiting around like this. There's bound to be Messican lawmen taking up the trail by now."

The big unshaven man grinned and winked at a lanky, older man who had his hat tipped down, his back to an up-ended saddle. "Told you she'd worry for the rest of us, Jake." The

older man ignored Deuce to say,
"She's right, Toke. We're not *that* far
yet. We'd be better off keepin' on the
trail at least until we get into them
mountains. I told you that yesterday ... One more thing, Toke ..."
The saturnine-faced older man finally
glanced at Deuce. There was not a
shred of anything at all in his cold
regard of her. "There wasn't nothing
said about no woman going along with
us when he figured out this raid."

To Blevins, the oaken younger man
did not look like someone to lightly
start an argument with. Then he rolled
closer to the base of his sheltering
bush for a closer look in Jake's
direction, and got a shock. He had
seen that lined, angular lean face on
wanted dodgers for some years. Jake
Kandelin, wanted for horsetheft, coach
and bank robbery, and also for murder.

Jake was the one man, Blevins
decided, who *could* pick an argument

with that oaken younger man. The other two were strangers to him but their value rose steadily as soon as Blevins identified Jake Kandelin. Whether there were also posters out on Arch and Toke, or not, simply the fact that they were in the company of Jake Kandelin lent them a degree of outlaw prestige Blevins was perfectly willing to concede to them.

Now though, after Kandelin had made that remark about Deuce, it seemed that the large younger man could lay down the law, even to Jake.

"I told you before we even come down here, Jake, that I knew a lady in Muletown who'd help, and she sure as hell has."

"We had supplies," growled Jake.

"Supplies!" scoffed the big man. "Tinned sardines and stuff like that. Look at the grub she brought us—and more tobacco. She goes along, Jake!"

Blevins held his breath. Without even looking at Kandelin's deadly face he knew from the posters that Jake was a killer at the drop of a hat.

Then Jake looked away, spat amber, shrugged thin shoulders and resumed his steady, unblinking study of their little smokeless fire.

Arch, whose back was fully to Blevins so that the lawman could not even see his profile, blew out a big noisy sigh and said, "We talked about this too, gents. No fightin' amongst us." Arch lifted the coffeepot and held it out. "Ma'm ... ?"

Clearly Arch was the peacemaker in this trio. He filled Deuce's cup and resettled the pot, then fished inside his shirt for a crooked little black Mex cigar which he lit with a great flourish—and that time Blevins saw his face.

Arch had thick, coarse features and bad teeth, but his little eyes were sunk-set like the eyes of a hawk and seemed not to miss a thing his companions did. When Deuce thanked him and smiled, Arch nodded but did not smile back.

The big man hunkered near the fire, poked at some meat in a little iron skillet, eyed Jake a time or two, and finally picked up a bottle of whisky, said, "Hey Jake!," and tossed it over.

Thus was peace among them re-established.

Blevins knew all he had to know. He began to very carefully work clear, sliding backwards in the dust as though he were a retreating side-winder, and when he was clear of the brush he got to his feet and without bothering to shake off dirt, turned to make the same big sashay out and around on his retreat as he had made to get up here in the first place.

Discovery now would ruin everything so with sweaty and infinite care he picked each footstep using up twice as much time reaching his horse as he had used earlier.

There was little chance of being

discovered. Those three renegades were engrossed in their own little drama back there. Blevins might have aroused them with noise but that was the one thing he was particularly careful not to do.

The horse was sleeping when he reached it, and opened one eye to watch for a moment before opening the other eye and becoming reconciled to another long ride.

They left the oat-grass clearing heading south-easterly in the direction of Muletown. Blevins had all the time in the world to sift through the alternatives which were available to him.

He knew how to make up the posse with which to run down those renegades, and he knew the route, the speed, and the methods to be used in getting over closer to the foothills for the capture.

Just one thing bothered him as he loped along. If Deuce was with them when the possemen fanned out for the interception she could very easily be killed because without a doubt men like Jake Kandelin would not surrender without a fight.

If she came home instead, if only in order to pick up the things she would need on the trail, it would simplify things. Blevins loped along hoping she would indeed visit Muletown at least once more, not because he wanted to confront her and make an apprehension but because no matter what he had ever personally thought of Deuce Farragut he had no stomach at all for seeing her get shot to death.

9

INTO THE NIGHT

The outlaws had mentioned heading for the distant mountains by nightfall, so when Sheriff Blevins got back to town in mid-afternoon he wasted just enough time to make certain his horse would be cared for, then he went over to the Mex cafe for something to eat, and took a tray across to the jailhouse with him.

When Leland started up his customary disagreeable conversation Blevins levelled a finger through the bars and said, "You son of a bitch, you got yourself in here, I didn't, so now you take the meals that come your way—and like it!"

Farragut looked surprised. He took

the tray to his bunk, turned to eye
Blevins again and said, "Well, all
right. But it seems to me when a
feller's locked up in here and helpless
and all, it'd be the responsibility——"

"Let me tell you where I've been,
Leland. Out at the sump-spring where
the old mud house is north-west of
town maybe six, seven miles."

"So you rode out there."

"Shut your stupid mouth and listen.
I followed your wife out there. Yesterday she bought a big stock of pro-
visions, plus plenty of tobacco. You
told me she didn't smoke. Then what
in hell did she need all that tobacco
for? She met three renegades at that
sump-spring. They are raiders who
killed some Mexicans down below the
line and raided a big ranch—robbed
the house."

Farragut had turned in violent
anger at first, now he was standing
and staring.

"She figures to leave with them.

With one of them anyway, a big strong-looking young buck called Toke. I came back here to make up a posse. Why am I telling you this? Because if she don't come back here before dark so's I can nab her, if she rides with those three renegades and we find them over against the mountains, Deuce could damned easily get herself killed. I wanted you to know that—and one other thing. She had no intention of coming to see you in here."

Farragut still stood like a carved image made of granite. Then he said, "Toke Mailer."

Blevins had not believed Leland knew the one called Toke. "Who is he?"

"Him and a couple other fellers come by couple weeks back. I never knew Toke very well but Deuce did. She'd known him, so she said anyway, back in Missouri. That's all. They just come by."

Leland stepped to the wall of his

cell and leaned with a noticeably, heavy slump. He looked away from Blevins and swore dully.

Blevins could not spend much more time here so he started to turn as he said, "See you later."

Leland did not seem to realise Blevins was leaving.

In the front office Blevins hunted up one of the dodgers on Jake Kandelin, sifted through none too thoroughly for dodgers on the other two, did not find them, pocketed the poster in his hand and went out locking the door after himself.

The sunlight was on a slanting angle by the time he crossed the road, buttonholed Arnold in the front of the general store, and said, "Posse. We'll meet at the liverybarn in fifteen minutes. You'd best fetch along your jacket and some grub; we'll be out all night."

He turned and walked briskly away. Ferguson stood about as Leland

Farragut had stood, gazing after the lawman with absolutely no approval and very little liking.

Blevins rounded up the gunsmith, who was a good man on a posse-ride, the saddle-maker who was also young and tough and willing, and finally he scouted up the saloon for rangeriders, but it was either too early in the day or too early in the week, but in any case there were only three or four itinerant rangemen hanging along the bar so Blevins gave it up. He had an idea in the back of his mind about passing close enough to Horton's cowcamp, or maybe sending someone back down there, to recruit additional men.

The critical point right now was to get moving.

They were ready to ride, all but Arnold Ferguson who only stalked up after the others had rigged out a horse for him and were in their saddles.

Arnie would not even look at Jim Blevins.

Each six months they made up a list of available men for posse duty. It was one of those civic things folks had to do. No one—very few people anyway—gladly rode out on armed manhunts.

Even those who did not object on moral grounds, were likely to object on the grounds that manhunting was a real hardship; they rode hard, fought hard sometimes, and covered considerable territory without decent meals nor a change of clothing, nor even a shave. Possemen in pursuit of renegades were ultimately reduced to the same desperate kind of furtive existence. No sane man liked that part of it, and those such as the gunsmith and saddle-maker who were young and tough enough to do it handily, did it because they earned a dollar a day. Purely and simply that was their reason. Most cowboys rode for the same reason—for the pay.

Ferguson's idealism always got in the way, but he had agreed when the list had been circulated. Like most other townsmen, he believed in civic service. He just did not really expect to be called on, so now as they jogged up through town and people stared because carbine-armed riders with a blanket, jackets, and saddlebags bulging with food were clearly man-hunters, Ferguson looked more morose than any of the others.

Blevins understood. At least to the extent that he chose to have no conversation with the storekeeper for the first hour or so.

He was sure a hell of a long way from being bereft over Arnie's dilemma. Riding ahead and setting the pace, he also had to guess about where those outlaws might try to enter the up-ended foothills, things which occupied him fully. Even if he'd had the time to agonise with Arnie he would not have done it. Jim Blevins was a pragmatic man. Most lawmen had to be, on the south desert or maybe anywhere else.

They remained on the stageroad up to the area of the rocks where Lee Farragut had made his sorry attempt at becoming a stage-robber. From there Blevins led off on an angling easterly route with the darkening foothills still a considerable distance onward.

The gunsmith was rawboned and hook-nosed. He had been several things including a lawman before settling on the south desert. Blevins had never enquired into the man's past. He never did that with anyone, so the only way he knew the gunsmith, whose name was Cliff Arden, had once served the law was from what Arden had voluntarily disclosed. Now, as they rode together scanning the distant foothills, the gunsmith said, "If

those men were at that sump-spring
where the old jacal was this morning,
and they figured to break camp and
head for them mountains this evening,
the way I got it figured, Sheriff, they
could darn easy be just about paral-
leling us, only westward maybe a
couple of miles. Thing is—who reaches
the foothills first?"

"We do," stated Blevins, who had
considered this even before leaving
town. "If we don't get up in there
ahead of them, they'll get through us
like water out of a tin horn, and
afterwards we'll be down to trackin'
with them knowing darned well we're
back there."

The gunsmith found a plug, bit off
a corner, offered the tobacco, and
when Blevins curtly shook his head the
gunsmith stowed his plug and pointed
with an upraised rein-hand. "If we
make better time than we're makin'
now and can get to the northward
more, if they make camp shy of the

hills and we're above them we'd ought to be able to see their cookin' fire."

This too had already been worked out by Jim Blevins. It was in fact the reason they were on their present course towards the hills, so all he said was, "We'll find them, and when we do you want to keep a close watch because at least one of those fellers is wanted from Montana to Sonora and he'll blow you out of that saddle quicker'n you can say scat."

They made excellent time. By late evening they were beginning to feel the first uneven ground which preceded the lowest foothills. Blevins was unsure of it, but he felt that those raiders probably had not been able to get any closer to the mountains.

They halted in an oak bosque to dismount, loosen cinchas and have a smoke, or a chew for those who chewed their tobacco rather than smoked it, and stand in silent long contemplation of the country flowing darkly and distantly southward on all but the north side of them.

Ferguson stood hunched, hands shoved deep into jacket pockets looking as solemn as an owl when he said, "They don't have to go through here, do they, Jim? I mean, they could aim for the foothills more westerly than this."

It was a possibility. What made Blevins doubt it, was the way they had talked at their sump-spring camp while he had spied and eavesdropped on them. There had been something said about making good time, about heading straight for the mountains, about not wasting time. Those things coupled together inclined Blevins to believe the raiders would not go riding up and down the foothills looking for the easiest place to breach them, they would aim dead ahead and throw themselves into the mountains wherever they found a trail.

His idea had been to reach the

foothills in at least a reasonable approximation of the place where he thought the raiders would also reach them.

Whether he had done it or not, it was perhaps a little too soon to tell.

They still had fair visibility but the daylight was gone, or was almost gone; there were streaks of pale light upon the uppermost mountains. They too would shortly vanish. Then dusk would be thoroughly emplaced.

The saddle-maker strolled over to smile a little and to say something about fanning out and keeping quiet. He was of the opinion if they waited patiently enough they would see a campfire and he was probably correct. Blevins reflected upon a woman's reaction on a dark night; he had seen it happen before. Women instinctively wanted light at night. Deuce might offer to make a meal for the renegades just in order to get some light into the menacing darkness.

He acceded to the saddle-makers' idea and split them up, left and right but with strict orders not to make a sound, not to show a light nor permit a horse to nicker, and if they saw anything to converge upon the place where he now was.

The last of them to depart was Arnie Ferguson and he was pulling on gloves against the increasing chill as he said, "How many more months does the list run, Jim?"

Blevins stifled an irritable comment. "Help me out this time Arnie, and I'll scratch you off for the time left."

Ferguson picked up his reins and went walking away.

This was one of those times when Jim would have enjoyed a smoke. But he had no tobacco and did not really want to smoke badly enough to go hunt up someone with a sack and papers, so he let the horse droop behind him, hunkered in the increasing dusk and kept scanning the miles and miles of south desert country below him, and wondered which course Deuce had taken; had she first returned to town, or had she already had whatever she would need when she had arrived at the renegade camp this morning, in which case she would now be riding towards him along with her friend—or whatever he was—named Toke Mailer.

He thought back to Jake's objection to her. It was not unlike that bizarre attitude old-time seamen had had about women along on sailing cruises. It had been impersonal and strong, with Jake. Nor did Blevins believe the outlaw would relent even though he might not bring the subject up again. Probably wouldn't bring it up again because from what Blevins had observed, Toke was the unchallenged leader.

As for Toke, Jim Blevins could not really make much of an assessment. The only thing Toke had done which

had left Blevins with an impression
had been to face down Jake Kandelin.
Otherwise he was simply a large
young man, perhaps who had once
been a rangeman and who was now an
outlaw. That he was bold and deadly
scarcely needed verifying; anyone who
with only two companions would go
down into the Province of Sonora and
attack the home-place of one of those
feudal Mex *rancheros*, had to be abun-
dantly supplied with courage.

The rest of it of course was that he
had brought it off successfully and
that said something for his sagacity
too.

But Blevins kept returning to Deuce.
Why in God's name did so handsome
a woman have to turn out like this?

But this was a subject Blevins
wisely forced himself away from. He
was by nature a gallant man. Too
much gallantry however turned into
something else. He was out here to
catch her right along with those

desperadoes she had encouraged and supplied. He did not like the idea at all, but this was not the first time the law had forced him into a situation which he found personally distasteful. It probably would not be the last time.

Someone slipping almost soundlessly in among the shadows and undergrowth to one side attracted his attention. He turned without arising, and not until he could make out Ferguson did he stand up.

Arnie said nothing as he walked on up but he pointed with a gloved hand so that Blevins would follow out the direction he was aiming. All Jim saw was more darkness. That's what he told Ferguson so the storekeeper dropped his arm and beckoned, heading over more to the east a few yards, and that time when he pointed Blevins saw it. A flickering little campfire down through the dead of the chilly night not only southward but also at least half a mile more eastward than Blevins would have expected it.

In fact his doubt was so strong he mentioned it. "Maybe some travellers, Arnie. It's closer to the stageroad than I figure they'd be—the ones we're after."

Ferguson humped up heavy shoulders inside his jacket and stood peering out there for a while, then said, "Maybe, Jim, but it's asking a hell of a lot of a coincidence—the one night we're up here manhunting, the one night fugitives are up through here somewhere heading for the mountains." He looked around. "Care if I have a look?"

In Blevins's view it was not a matter of 'caring' as much as it was a matter of worrying over Arnie's ability at something like this, so he said, "Take your horse over where we left my critter, and stay there. If the other fellers come along tell them where I'm going. All right?"

Evidently Ferguson had not been keen on scouting up that camp because he briskly nodded in acquiescence, then without another word turned and walked off leaving Blevins to stand a while fixing the location of that fire in mind before striking out towards it.

He was not convinced it might be their fugitives right up until he got within listening distance and heard the soft-fluting tones of an unmistakable female voice. He probably should have turned back right then, but it was his nature to make absolutely certain about something like this, so he continued onward, finally made out hobbled horses below camp a short distance and curved far out so that he'd be able to approach the animals from the south, which was downwind.

The voices were still distinguishable but not the words. Men's voices all sounded pretty much the same to Blevins even in broad daylight and even when they were no farther than rooms' distance away, but this particular female voice. ...

A horse nickered, Blevins dropped flat, and over at that little campfire everyone went silent.

Blevins did not have time to swear. He did not even have time to feel like swearing. Shortly now someone was bound to come out from the camp so he concentrated on slithering back into the underbrush, to keep right on crawling even after he heard a man say, "Swift-fox most likely."

A second voice said, "Band of coyotes maybe." Then this man, whose voice was dry as dust, also said, "Arch, for now things is all right, but Toke don't get no credit, and when the trail gets hot I don't want to be around him moonin' at that long-legged woman."

Arch had an uneasy reply to offer. "Yeah, but we been partners and he's never even got close to bein' caught yet, Jake. I don't like watchin' him and her neither. This is a race for life even if it don't much seem like it, and he's actin' like we're on a church picnic."

"Then you're ready to take our share and split off?"

Arch turned to head back towards the camp as he said, "I told you—we been partners. No, I'm not ready to split up and ride off."

Jake said no more as the pair of them headed for camp. Blevins arose gingerly and picked thornpins out of his arms where he had inadvertently and in haste brushed a big thicket.

He had all the verification that would be required so as he continued to pick out stickers he walked back.

It was a considerable distance. Farther than he had expected, and when he got over there the other three men were waiting. There was some blood on his sleeve from some of the thornpin punctures which he was dabbing at when he saw the possemen on ahead.

Ferguson said, "Well?"

"It's the renegades and Deuce is with them. Anyone got the makings?"

The gunsmith spat amber and shook his head but the saddle-maker offered papers and tobacco. While they waited, Blevins recounted what he had worked out in his mind on the walk back.

"Too risky going down there now. If we spook 'em and they scatter, even on foot, without no moon and darn little starshine we're going to lose 'em. We'll leave our horses over here and walk down a little ways, then set and wait. When it's light enough to see we'll slip in on their camp."

He finished with the punctured arm. It was beginning to itch, which was the invariable aftermath of getting stuck by those particular thorns.

No one said a word so they went over to make certain the horses were safely secured, and when they came back each man was carrying his carbine and Arnie had removed the blanket from behind his saddle and had it looped over one shoulder, across his body and tied at one hip like a Confederate soldier. Arnie did not like the cold. Neither did the others but they had not gone to that extreme to avoid it.

Blevins turned to lead the way.

10

BY STEALTH!

Among four possemen there was not a watch, so when they got over where Blevins thought it would be safe to wait, and tried to guess how long they might have to wait before dawnlight returned, the estimates ranged from five hours to three hours, a variance which probably would not have been so wide if there had been a moon, but all they had to go by in the darkness was starlight and guesswork, two unreliable bases.

Blevins was tired. It had been a very long day before he had even left town with his posse, and that had been hours earlier. Tiredness promoted forgetfulness, so it was said, and perhaps that was why Blevins had overlooked the little diversion on his way up here to stop by Harry Horton's cow-camp for additional recruits.

He thought of that now, speculated on how much time they had, if he sent someone back down there to bring up several more riders, and decided that if he could keep the advantage of surprise he would not need a small army. As it was, his posse outnumbered the renegades.

He also decided they should rest for an hour or two, and suggested this. He had one more thing to do before they hit the renegades but he wanted a little rest first. He meant to put those outlaws on foot before sunrise, and as he burrowed against the chilly earth to sleep for a short while he thought back to the locality of the stolen loose-stock, and one moment later before he could plan further, he fell dead asleep.

Arnie Ferguson shook his head. "I've seen him do this before," he told the other two possemen. "Stretch out and sleep like this."

Cliff Arden the gunsmith gazed at Blevins's dark form against the ground. "I don't see nothin' wrong with it. A feller gets wore down and he's got to rest. That's all."

Ferguson stared. "Right here; within rifle-range of a band of murdering renegades?"

The saddle-maker sided with the gunsmith. "In his kind of business I'd say a man's likely to sleep somewhere near outlaws no matter when he flops down." Then the saddle-maker also had another observation to put forth. "If that damned Lee Farragut's long-legged woman is down there, and there's trouble, and she maybe sides in with them outlaws—what do we do?"

"Shoot her," said the gunsmith without a moment's hesitation. He did not elaborate and the other two men gazed at him in solid silence. He saw their looks and ignored them. He was clearly a realistic individual; the sex of someone with a gun aimed in his direction had nothing at all to do with it. He had a cud of chewing tobacco in his mouth and went right ahead rhythmically chewing it as he lifted out a beautifully-balanced Colt .45 with stag grips and considered the load-butts in each round of the cylinder. The gun was fully charged. Evidently the gunsmith did not believe in keeping an empty casing beneath the hammer, a practice some rangemen employed against the possibility that in a fall or other kind of accident a gun might accidentally discharge and seriously injure its owner.

They ate in dogged silence, their meal meagre but adequate. It was also tasteless, which was another odd thing about situations like this; men waiting to fight perhaps for their lives, did not seem able to taste food very well.

They were still eating when Blevins rolled over, sat up and yawned, then swung his arms because the chill had been increasing for some time now. Arnie silently offered half a tin of peaches. Just as soundlessly the sheriff accepted, tipped the can and first drank the syrup, then went to work on the can's contents. When he finished he arose and said, "Couple of us got to get their horses." He pointed at the gunsmith. "You and me, Cliff."

Arden did not hesitate, he simply asked whether they should haul along their saddle-guns and Blevins shook his head. If there was to be any shooting, by the time he and Cliff Arden got down that close, it would be hand-gun work. Also, carbines were a nuisance unless they were definitely to be used; they kept one of a man's hands tied up.

Ferguson said, "Just the two of you, Jim?"

Blevins nodded his head. "That ought to be enough, Arnie. You fellers keep watch. Whatever happens down there, stay out of it unless it comes up here." He dryly smiled at the squatting storekeeper. "I'd sure hate to get shot by one of you boys."

Cliff Arden was one of those men it was a delight to have along in most situations. If he had fear it did not show, and he accepted what they were out to do with total equanimity where men like Arnold Ferguson had a habit of being sceptical most of the time.

The gunsmith was also younger than Arnie, and a lot rougher and tougher. As he and the lawman started southward amidst a dark world of brush-shapes and shadows Arden said, "Where are the horses?"

Blevins gestured. "They're hobbled so they won't be where I last saw them, but out in that direction somewhere." In anticipation of the next question he widened his gesture. "And the renegades got their camp yonder. If they got a watcher out we might run into trouble."

Arden grinned. "Yeah, we might."

It was cooler out away from the foothills but to men moving right along that posed no problem. What bothered Blevins more was the noise those horses were going to make when—and if—they were freed to run off. He wished he knew how much darkness they had left.

Arden spoke up as though he had just read the sheriff's mind. "Be daylight by my calculations in another hour and a half."

Blevins scanned the eastern rims, but if the gunsmith were right there was no indication of it over there. Nevertheless, Jim picked up the gait a little, and because they had to go around the area where they finally detected vagrant scents of campfire coals, it seemed they were going to have to cover considerable ground before they even found the horses.

That proved correct, as did Blevins's suspicion that the horses had

moved away from where he had first
sighted them.

It was Cliff who saw them, finally.
He was a yard or two wide of his
companion and over the tops of some
low blue-sage something moved back
and forth as it picked sage-buds.
Arden stopped dead still, eluded
detection by the horse, which was odd,
then as the animal turned to one side
to either see where his companions
were, or perhaps to find another blue-
sage bush, Cliff Arden slipped over to
Blevins, nudged him and led the way
from this point on.

Four horses and three of them were
hobbled. The fourth horse was already
free to leave if it chose to, except that
it was a mare with the stronger crowd-
instincts than existed in geldings, so
she remained within seeing and hearing
distance of the three hobbled geldings.
Blevins pointed to the grulla without
comment. If Arden understood what
that signified he did not let on. He was

more concerned in how they were to get out there without causing the horses to snort or perhaps go madly hopping away. A horse who understood hobbles could hop on his restricted front legs almost as fast as some horses could slow-lope.

Blevins played a hunch, he left the gunsmith waiting in the underbrush and eased gently ahead in the direction of the grulla. Only a couple of nights ago, as well as the previous night, he had left his scent where the grulla had unmistakably detected it. This was the thinnest kind of basis for familiarity now, many miles northward, but it had to be better than no basis at all.

He also knew something of the grulla's temperament. The horse was not easily upset nor frightened, so when he finally emerged from the underbrush he started talking his way up, and the horse lifted his head to watch and listen.

The other three horses did not realise for a while what was happening, but when they too picked up man-scent, they turned to stare.

Blevins was distant from them, so whatever their feelings they had no need to be frightened—yet.

The grulla finally lifted its head and braced for the moment when Blevins reached a gentle hand to stroke its neck. The horse nuzzled the man, sniffed, pushed his long face forth to do additional sniffing, and Blevins turned to gesture Cliff Arden forward. If one or two loose horses bolted, once they were free, there was a good chance the remaining hobbled horses might attempt the same thing with disastrous results for the men out there in the menacing night. What Blevins wanted was for all four horses to bolt at the same time. He left Arden stroking the grulla's neck and approached the nearest of the Mexican horses, a leggy bay with the crest and head and eyes of a thoroughbred. This horse was definitely high-strung but like most horses raised and handled from colthood by horsemen rather than cowmen, he did not fear even a stranger in the darkness.

Blevins stroked his way down to the big bay's ankles, looked back, saw Cliff also kneeling at ground level, and Jim eased off the plaited rawhide hobbles of the big bay. He promptly headed for the next horse.

That loose mare was the only one which offered problems. She was clearly 'horsing' and that made her objectionable to the geldings so they had evidently nipped her a time or two, in this strictly horsey way letting her know they did not want her very close, but with men around the mare became bold and walked back.

Blevins had not quite freed one hobble on the last animal when the silly mare edged up to the leggy bay. Without warning he shot back his little ears, threw forth his head and snapped with huge white teeth. The mare squealed even though she had been quick enough to escape that savage lunging bite, but as she whirled, that action frightened the other horses. The animal where Blevins was kneeling gave no warning that he was going to move. He simply grunted and sprang ahead bowling Blevins over and over. The horse leapt the tumbling man, lit down on all four hooves, discovered there was one flopping hobble, and as though this frightened him anew, he ran with an abrupt burst of speed which inspired the sudden same reaction in the other horses.

In a twinkling the ground reverberated to all those simultaneous sounds of large horses thundering overland in a panicked group.

Cliff Arden dashed over where Blevins was groggily trying to arise, caught hold of the lawman's jacket and almost bodily hoisted Jim to his feet. He then propelled the lawman in the direction of the closest large stand of flourishing underbrush. Behind them somewhere a man's heartfelt and deep-down profanity rattled through the echoing night.

Blevins had trouble recovering his breath. There was no sensation of pain, yet, but he knew the horse had hit him in the chest with its knees as it had lunged ahead knocking him over.

The gunsmith palmed his Colt and eased in close to the base of a bush peering out and around. Evidently, though, the aroused renegades were nowhere nearly as concerned with where their horses had been as they were concerned with where their horses were going. It did not seem, right at this time, that the renegades had begun to wonder how all those horses had worked free of the hobbles at the same time, but Blevins, leaning forward, hands on knees, fighting to hasten full recovery from nearly having his wind knocked out, was less concerned with the side-effects of his act than he was in getting back northward. He forced himself to stand erect, hissed for Cliff to return, then started none too steadily to walk away.

Arden came up and leaned to look, but Blevins had his breath back by this time. He also was beginning to have a noticeable pain in the chest, which he attempted to ignore as he growled for the gunsmith to hasten.

Somewhere to their right a man sang out and was answered directly by another man. The renegades were making a very definite attempt to recapture their horses, which meant of course that unless they ultimately returned to their camp there was a fair chance they might still get free.

Blevins was satisfied on that score, for even if they caught the horses, and even if it occurred to them finally that those hobbles had *not* come free by themselves, the renegades still had all

their loot as well as their horse-gear
and personal gatherings at the camp.

11

TROUBLE!

Arnie and the saddle-maker were figuratively hopping from foot to foot by the time Arden and the sheriff returned. Arnie pointed eastward. He had heard the horses over in that direction, but oddly neither he nor the saddle-maker had heard those men shouting to one another.

Blevins knew he had been hit. The breathing impairment was no longer relevant but that pain near the breastbone was solidly there, so as he spoke he kept a hand inside his jacket without thinking about doing that.

"We can use what's left of the night to get a lot closer now that they're scattered out and thinkin' mostly about their livestock."

He gestured, the other men moved to fan out a little, then the stealthy advance was renewed, southward. Arden kept watching the sheriff. He did not know how hard Blevins had been hit but he knew Jim had been hurt.

If Blevins had been sleepy that pain in the chest would have taken his mind off it. As it was, while he watched the others spread out, he continued to massage his chest inside the jacket. If that accomplished much it was not immediately noticeable.

They utilised the underbrush as though they were stalking Apaches. Blevins was satisfied that even if all three of the renegades had gone after the horses, there would still be one gun left down there—Deuce Farragut's gun.

She remained the unknown quotient and Blevins did not want to think about her as he gestured for his companions to follow his example.

They finally felt rather than saw that the purple darkness was beginning to soften towards a diluted form of grey-blue. With this dawning change there was a continuation of the late-night hush which had prevailed so long now they hardly remembered when there had been noise.

Someone out ahead had placed fresh tinder upon the fire. It sputtered to an uneven and raggedy brightness in an otherwise unlit world. Clearly, then, someone had not joined in the horse-hunt. Clearly too, whoever that was at the camp did not realise those horses getting free had not been just bad luck.

The stalking possemen advanced more cautiously, but now they had something to concentrate upon. It only occurred to Blevins after some little time that he might be walking into a trap or, worse yet, leading his friends into one.

It seemed such a remote possibility that he continued on course for another dozen yards before deciding to take a fresh precaution. He wigwagged in the cold pre-dawn for his possemen to hang back, then he started ahead alone, but angling in such a manner as to never be without heavy underbrush in front.

He slipped in and out in the maze of underbrush until he could actually hear the crackling, then straightened up in all stealth and leaned to part some bush-limbs.

The camp was in the same kind of disarray that other camp had been in, and although he had a good look at it, thanks to the little fire in the centre of the small clearing, he did not see anyone out there.

He waited for what seemed a long while and when no one emerged he turned back to find his possemen.

They were waiting and strongly curious, carbines slung over bent arms. He explained, the men surmised the renegades would return, no matter where they now were, so the advance was undertaken again, but this time Blevins knew exactly where to take them.

They had plenty of time to get into position. In fact Cliff Arden yawned, scratched a bristly cheek, and ruefully grinned at Jim Blevins as though to say the delay was boring him. Maybe it was, but boredom did not appear to be Arnie Ferguson's worry. He was belly-down in his old jacket, carbine pushed ahead as though an entire army of foemen were to shortly appear and engage him.

The silence lingered. If anything, rather then lighten as daylight approached, in this particular place it seemed to deepen.

Blevins crept a yard onward, parted the vines again and looked out there.

The temptation was strong to visit the deserted camp. Without a doubt he could obtain sufficient incriminating material from those *alforjas*. On the other hand by being prudent he would get the same evidence and along with it, perhaps, some renegades.

Then a man's loud call far to the east ended Blevins's thoughts of slipping out there. He looked left and right. The other men tightened up their faces, settled more solidly in hiding, and waited.

Blevins was curious to know whether or not the renegades had captured the horses. He did not have to wait long for his answer.

The outlaw named Arch Murray appeared, hatless and trailing an unused lariat from one shoulder. He was fully dressed but no rangeman looked fully attired without his hat. Nor did most of them feel right, without their top-piece.

Four sets of eyes watched Arch

without winking. Like Apaches, the possemen remained totally blended with their environment, utterly still and deadly. Also like Apaches, who almost never struck on the first sighting, the possemen crouched ready and willing, but in no evident haste.

Arch filled a tin cup from the little coffeepot, sipped and looked around, flung down his lariat and sipped more coffee. He looked completely disgruntled.

He also looked very susceptible to capture—except that even loud voices at this juncture would carry out where there could very easily be more renegades. Blevins decided to use Arch as bait.

The wait was nerve-racking. It was also very prolonged. Arnie was the first one to fidget, next came the saddle-maker. Blevins controlled himself with an effort and the rhythmically chewing gunsmith seemed the least nervous of the lot. He half-smiled as he watched Arch over there drinking coffee. Arden masticated his cud, and waited.

A man called from over in the direction from which Arch had materialised. "Hey! You at the fire: Toke?"

That had been Jake Kandelin. Blevins recognised the dryness, the almost total lack of inflection in the killer's voice.

Arch answered without looking away from his coffee. "It's me, Jake. Toke isn't back yet ... Jake; you get a horse?"

Kandelin answered in a manner which brought every posseman wide awake in a second. "No horse and we ain't goin' to get them back neither. They was deliberately set free and stampeded ... Hey, Arch; you better get away from that fire!"

For two or three seconds Arch Murray sat still looking slowly from left to right. Then he abruptly dropped the tin cup, sprang upright and made the most disastrous mistake of his life; instead of running to the right or the left, or even ducking back into the underbrush behind him from which he had emerged so shortly ago, he sprang across the fire and hurled himself straight at the underbrush where the possemen were waiting. It may have been closer but it definitely was more hazardous.

Even so he moved with such sudden speed he almost made it. He was across the fire heading almost directly towards the place where Blevins was waiting, gun in hand, when Cliff Arden, who was to the left of Jim Blevins, dropped his carbine and jumped up aiming his body for a wild tackle.

The two men connected with a grunt of breath knocked out of Arden but it evidently had no effect because the gunsmith caught cloth in both hands and hung on, dragging Arch Murray to the ground when Cliff fell.

Murray was a solidly put-together man, oaken in his strength and because the life he led did not allow a man to get soft, he was almost as much as the more sedentary and taller gunsmith could handle even though Arden had the initial advantage.

Blevins scuttled over there to swing his sixgun like a club. He did not want the outlaw to recover from astonishment and yell. But that same thought had occurred to Arnie Ferguson whose big body looked even bigger inside his jacket as he pushed back and struggled to his feet to head for the rolling, battling individuals.

Murray aimed a knee for Arden's groin. It got deflected by a knee. Murray struck furiously with both flailing strong arms and this time Arden, who was clutching cloth with one hand could not throw up much protection. But he buried his face against the renegade and continued to stubbornly hang on with one hand while trying hard to land a good strike with the other hand. He hit Murray a number of times but because he could not see his aim was bad.

Murray suddenly arched with all his strength, broke clear and rolled to get all four limbs squarely beneath so he could jump up. Arden aimed a wild kick, connected with Murray's right side and knocked the renegade sideways. After that, Cliff had the advantage and never relinquished it again. He jumped, landed atop the outlaw, buried his face again and went to work with both big fists pummelling as hard as he could against the unprotected soft parts of the renegade. Murray gasped from pain, tried to throw Cliff Arden off, then made his second bad error, he jerked upright, head and shoulders, to force Arden's face into the clear, and the scheme backfired when Cliff could see upwards, aimed a powerful right fist, connected along the point of the outlaw's jaw, and the fight was over just as both Blevins and Ferguson were in position to knock Murray over the head.

Blevins dropped to one knee to make certain Murray did not cry out. It was an unnecessary precaution. When the gunsmith's fist sledged into Murray's jaw the renegade had no time to even form an outcry let alone get one off before he lost consciousness.

They helped Arden to his feet. He wiped his knuckles along a shirtfront and flexed them. They had been bruised and were faintly bleeding. Arden was also almost completely out of breath. Working at a gunsmith's vice and bench day in and day out did little to keep a man in shape.

But Cliff grinned at the others and softly said, "When I first saw him I figured on the spur of the moment he

was a little guy ... Little like a little
grizzly bear!"

Arnie Ferguson who was even larger than Arden, gazed at the unconscious outlaw as though he might aver
that Murray was indeed not very
large, but in the end Arnie kept his
mouth closed.

They gagged their first captive,
bound him securely with his own two
belts, his britches-belt and his shellbelt, then rolled him to one side as
someone to the south of them called
from a considerable distance. This
time, Blevins was sure of the voice.
Toke Mailer was returning, and when
he called forth it was to announce that
he had two horses and needed help
bringing them in.

Blevins made up his mind on the
spot and said, "Come along; that's the
one we don't want to let get away."

They left Arch Murray and struck
out southward, but on an angling
course which would eventually put

them between Toke Mailer and the camp. That way they would be certain to intercept him. That way, too, Blevins was sure, had to be roughly where Jake Kandelin had been when he had warned Murray, back a few minutes.

Blevins made the others cautious by his example as they headed southward. There was still the possibility of surprising the renegades even though it appeared that at least Kandelin had surmised the renegades were not the only ones abroad in the night.

It would have helped a lot, would at least have done something for Jim Blevins's peace of mind, if Jake had called out again. Blevins had thought he might, after Toke had yelled ahead, but clearly Kandelin had not lived to reach middle age as an outlaw by doing what possemen expected him to do.

The danger of stumbling over Kandelin as they all headed down where

Toke Mailer had called from worried Blevins more and more. He still viewed Jake as the most deadly of the raiders; probably as the most deadly outlaw riding the backtrails of the Territory, in fact.

It was this concentration on Kandelin which allowed them all to commit an oversight. Without warning, Deuce Farragut ran into an opening dead ahead of them holding a carbine in both hands as though she knew the lawmen were close by. They had one chance to drop before she whirled in their direction, but she was whirling completely around, clearly in a state of near panic although it did not seem she could have known of their presence—yet, anyway—so she continued to whirl. Maybe poor lighting along with her evident fright also helped, but in any case the men were prone about sixty yards distant and she did not seem to have seen them at all.

She stopped moving, slowly emerged from her crouch, slowly lowered the carbine and seemed to Jim to be trying to recover her breath as though she had been running. She was much too distant to be successfully run down and grabbed—she was also too heavily armed for anyone to try that. Blevins could have downed her with one shot. So could the other possemen but even Cliff Arden who had expressed no qualms earlier did not now raise his firearm in her direction.

She suddenly vanished. One moment she was there, at the far distant side of the large opening, the next moment she had seemed to vanish into the air, but what she had done was step directly around a large bush and drop from sight. Now, finally, the gunsmith whispered heartfelt curses and struggled clear of his protective under-brush to lunge upright and swiftly go trotting to the west, a yard or two, until he also vanished.

Blevins could have shouted for him

not to go after her and if he'd done
that he would have betrayed the
posse's presence to Kandelin and
Mailer. Nonetheless the temptation
was very strong. It was the saddle-
maker's dry whisper which made the
difference.

"If anyone can catch her from
behind it's Cliff."

They were still engrossed with this
affair when Toke Mailer called ahead
again, much closer now and sounding
annoyed because no one had respon-
ded to his earlier outcry. It struck
Blevins that although the big youthful
renegade had captured two of the
freed horses and must certainly must
have wondered at them being loose
without hobbles at the same time, he
was not acting very prudent as he
headed noisily for the camp.

They could have remained in place
but Blevins was worried over the
gunsmith heading directly into the
area where two renegade killers were,

along with Deuce Farragut, so he cursed under his breath and led out.

Now, whatever the oucome, they were going to lose their advantage shortly so Blevins quietly picked up speed and motioned for his companions to spread out again.

The dawnlight had been slowly but perceptibly brightening without anyone actually noticing it now that contact with the renegades had been made, until Arnie gasped, stepped swiftly into the shadow of a big bush and pointed ahead where Blevins saw a man's head and shoulders appear, jerkily, then disappear.

It happened so fast he could not even be sure it had been Toke Mailer but it certainly laid emphasis upon the fact that visibility was now adequate while also emphasising the proximity of the converging enemies.

12

SUNRISE AND BEYOND

Someone fired a carbine in the cold dawn. Blevins winced in spite of himself, but clearly whoever that was on ahead a reasonable distance had not fired towards the men back northward.

A horse suddenly came charging up through the tall underbrush dodging left and right as he sped along. They could hear his approach so when he burst into their particular clearing each posseman was flattened back out of the way. It was Deuce Farragut's grulla gelding. It probably saw the strangers but offered no indication of it. Blevins caught one quick glimpse of streaked blood on the horse's rump, evidently where a bullet had raked along making a superficial but stinging wound.

The saddle-maker went over where the horse had come from and looked, then without taking his eyes off whatever he saw out there, he beckoned for the others to come on up beside him.

They did not quite make it. Kandelin's thin-edged, emotionless voice cried a warning and in the very next breath two gunshots came so close together they sounded like one prolonged explosion. The saddle-maker threw up a hand to shield his face and dropped to both knees.

Blevins thought he had been hit and ran to one side to look beyond and see where the gunman was. Arnie went over to the saddle-maker.

Now, the advantage was definitely gone. In a sense Blevins was glad of it. He was not a man of voluntary violence but once the inhibitions had been removed in this kind of situation he knew exactly how to react, and that simplified a lot of things.

Of course Deuce was still out there and that would have worried him except that when he got into the brush patch someone on the far side of it fired, cutting twigs on both sides of him. There was nothing to clear a man's head of other thoughts as quickly as a near-hit from a gun.

He ducked down and continued to bore ahead. He emerged into a tiny clearing, half straightened up, heard someone speak sharply to someone else out yonder, and ducked low to bore through another brushy place, and this time he caught a glimpse of someone— or some*thing*—and halted in a low crouch waiting and listening.

There was someone across the clearing. It was possibly two people. He could have fired, could perhaps have bracketed them and driven his third shot straight down the centre and hit one of them, instead he waited and did not move.

There was no sign of Toke nor the other horse, nor did he see any of his own possemen although at least two of them were still close by somewhere behind him.

A person was stealthily withdrawing over yonder. Blevins could keep track of their movements by watching the topmost chaparral limbs sway ever so gently.

A woman screamed. It was a sound pitched to a key of purest terror. Then she was drowned out by a gunshot and afterwards her voice did not carry into the wake of the long gunshot-echo.

Blevin had his teeth on edge as he started ahead. Cliff Arden was somewhere yonder, and whether Blevins approved of the way his posseman had run off on his own mission or not, Arden was closer to the outlaws than he should have been and that probably meant he needed help.

Left of the site where Blevins was emerging someone pitched a rock. As a ruse it was a failure. As a matter of fact for someone to expect a reaction to something that time-worn made Blevins wonder. He looked about where that rock had to have come from but there was no movement. Nonetheless he faded back into the underbrush and waited again.

A horse struggled, making it sound as though he had been tied and something had frightened him to make him sit back and pull.

Blevins used that diversion to step from one big bush to the one adjoining to the east a few yards. Then he came around the side of this bush and saw the clearing, which was larger than most clearings in this area, and upon the far side of it, sure enough there was a halter-pulling horse, only now the beast had come up his tether and was looking fearfully around. Whatever had spooked him, if it had been a visible thing, was nowhere around. At least Blevins did not see it as he sank to one knee in bush-shade and watched intently.

The silence was worse than the sound of gunfire. Blevins felt alone and menaced on all sides. Then he detected sounds, very furtive ones, behind him in the direction of the camp and eased around beginning to suspect that at least one of the renegades was not going to abandon the camp even though by now he certainly knew there were possemen around.

It was a little while before Blevins got back over there. The distance had not been great but he had not been able to make a direct approach either, so when he came close enough to where he and his possemen had first arrived nearby he could look from the base of a squat thornpin bush and have a good view.

The man out there was furiously

pawing through one of the Mex *alfor-jas*. He was sweatily hurling things left and right in frantic search of something. He had his sixgun holstered and his body, which was angular and sinewy, bent over as he furiously worked.

He plunged both hands deep, hung there briefly, then reared back and Blevins had his first view of the man's face. It was Jake Kandelin!

Blevins aimed and called out. "Jake! *Not a move!*"

Kandelin had two buckskin pouches in each hand. It was a mistake and he clearly knew it the moment Blevins accosted him. No matter how fast a gunman might be, he would never be fast enough to drop those pouches *then* draw. Not against an aimed gun and most likely not even against a leathered one.

Jake hung there. The clearing was not so wide he could not have tried running, but that may never have occurred to him as he loosened slightly in his stance and let the sacks sink to his sides without relinquishing them. He was staring in the general direction of Jim Blevins but evidently had been unable to make out exactly where the lawman was hiding.

"Turn around," Blevins said quietly. "Turn, Jake, and drop the pouches, then drop that sixgun."

Kandelin did not obey. He traced out the speckled outline of the prone man, stood looking with a deep frowning squint, then he said in his flat, inflectionless voice that he had four pouches of Mex gold and that he'd pitch two of those sacks across, and all Jim had to do was to turn his back for one minute.

Jim repeated his order. "Drop 'em and turn around then drop the gun!"

"You damned fool there is a fortune in gold here!" exclaimed the outlaw. "You'll punch cows until you're old as the hills and never make this much."

Jim tilted the gun-barrel. "I'm the law, not a rangeman," he exclaimed. "Jake, for the last time—drop 'em and the gun!"

Kandelin moved his feet slightly as he dropped the bullion pouches. Then he demonstrated the basic reason why he had been so successful outside the law for so long. He went for his gun as he twisted thinly sideways and took two rearwards steps. He made of himself the poorest target he could, and he was fast enough to get off one shot at Blevins, which was a shade too high, and to tip down the barrel with a thumbpad on the dog to cock his weapon for the second shot, before Jim fired.

Speed was desirable but not indispensable. Accuracy was much better and Jim Blevins had been aiming and waiting for ten seconds before he squeezed the trigger.

Jake Kandelin staggered, half turned away, fired into the earth fifty feet away, then fought to turn back as Jim fired again.

Jake Kandelin fell and flattened and did not move again.

Someone with a carbine fired southward. There were two immediate responses with handguns as though Jim's shot at Jake had set off a sequence. Then silence returned deeper than before.

Blevins backed clear, stood up, turned still holding the gun and called down there. "Arnie—Cliff ...?"

A strong voice called back. "Yo! Where are you, Sheriff?"

"At the camp ground. Where are you, Cliff?"

"South of there where someone tied a horse in the bushes. You nail one up there?"

"Yeah. You?"

"Yeah. I think it's that feller who brought back the horses."

Arnie called over to Cliff Arden. He

was much closer to Cliff than he was to Jim Blevins. "Where's the woman?"

Cliff answered almost indifferently. "Damned if I know but she ain't here I can tell you that."

Arnie did not reply and as Blevins turned away to go down there without so much as another glance out where Kandelin was lying, the sun's first warm rays began to slant downwards across all the vastness of the flat country, and even farther back, up where the foothills shaded off into darker and more formidable chains of peaks and pitches and brakes.

If Deuce were still around by now she knew what the magnitude of the disaster was. Jim was willing to believe she was hiding, or was perhaps slinking soundlessly away through the underbrush.

They could hunt her down.

He came upon the saddle-maker whom he had been sure had been shot in the face. What had happened was

that stinging bits of flying underbrush
had scratched his face and struck his
eyes.

He was able to see now but his eyes
were still teary and his scratched face
showed little flung-back streaks of
blood. He gazed at the lawman
without speaking, then turned and
they both went on through the underbrush until they located Arnie. He was
down there with Cliff Arden, and
another dead man. This time it was
the oaken big young man called Toke.
Toke Mailer. He still had a cocked
sixgun in his flung-back right fist
gripped as though it were his only
hope, which it may have been, but it
had been a forlorn hope.

When Arden saw Jim Blevins he
said, "I almost caught her, but just
when I was fixin' to jump over a brush
clump onto her, someone shot, and she
jumped out of sight in the darned
brush like a scairt rabbit." Arden
gestured. "Him? Well, he came

through that slot in the bushes yonder and when he saw me he must have figured I was one of his friends because he straightened up and started to say something. Then he saw his mistake." The gunsmith shrugged. "I shot the son of a bitch."

Arnie faintly frowned. "He was drawing?"

"Yeah," conceded the gunsmith, "but he couldn't have made it. I was already set for him. He did a darned stupid thing—he come walking up through there with his gun in the holster."

Arnie's frown deepened. "But hell, Cliff, he didn't know we were around here. Not at that moment. You could have called on him to throw it down."

Jim Blevins resented the storekeeper's criticism   he said, "Fat lot of good that might have done. I called on Kandelin to throw down—twice—and he still tried to kill me."

The saddle-maker was glumly

nodding as though he agreed with Blevins's imputation.

"What about the woman?" Arden asked. Then, before anyone could answer, he also said, "I could have nailed her nice as you please except that she got spooked and I never saw her again."

Blevins nodded; he had already heard that once before. Instead of speaking to the gunsmith he sent the saddle-maker back for their horses with an admonition to keep a close watch as he headed up there for although it seemed next to impossible that Deuce would have fled northward into the inhospitable mountains, there was a slim possibility.

"And she's armed, so keep close watch."

As the saddle-maker turned away Blevins gestured for Cliff to grab the boots of Toke Mailer while Blevins took his shoulders. Arnie walked ahead all the way back to their camp pushing aside underbrush.

The sun was climbing, the warmth was coming fresher and stronger, there were some dirty little fat clouds floating in from the north which no one noticed, and as Blevins went around to retrieve those four buckskin pouches someone saw Kandelin and softly whistled.

Arnie shed his jacket which was a certain sign that it was warm enough again. They all looked more villainous than a gang of genuine outlaws, being unshaven, dirty, rumpled and heavily armed, standing in the dishevelled renegade-camp with two dead men at their feet.

Ferguson went over to search for the renegade they had left tied and gagged. Cliff went back down to bring back that tethered horse.

Jim thought of a strong drink of whisky and turned to look around. What he turned up was a bottle two-thirds empty and with slobber stains around the mouth of it. He flung the bottle away, found an unopened sack of Bull Durham off someone's bedroll and made himself a smoke instead.

It was a poor substitute for breakfast but it did not taste as bad as it might have as he systematically went through the opened *alforja* then moved along to also open the other ones as well as the saddlebags on each upended rig. He found jewellery, more pouches of Mexican gold coins, some very old pieces of religious art, crucifixes, rosaries, jewelled inlaid tiny paintings of Catholic saints.

The rest of the plunder was valuable but it was mostly rare cloth, exquisite embroidered pieces, and a leather box of sterling silver dinnerware which was massive, clearly hand-wrought by a very talented craftsman, and that box was the heaviest item among the *alforjas.*

Blevins had no idea of the value of

all this loot except the gold coins and he did not right at that time take time to empty each pouch and count its contents. What he wanted now was to get out of here, get back down to Muletown. He did not even want to think about hunting the desert for Deuce.

Cliff Arden returned with the horse. Between them they rigged it out so that when the others got back they could load up and start back. Cliff looked at the debris and shook his head. "Why bring all that junk back; why not just gold and silver and jewellery?"

Blevins had no answer so he offered none.

Cliff found some cold coffee and would have fired up the little stone-ring fireplace if he had not heard horses coming from the north, and although both he and Jim were satisfied about that, after what they had just survived they were still enough on edge to wait until the saddle-maker hove into sight, and by then it was too late to make hot coffee.

Their horses looked good to men who had been on foot under circumstances which were a long way from being enviable for the shank of a deadly night and for the first part of a golden autumn morning.

13

THE ROAD BACK

Arch Murray stood dumbly gazing at the dead men. His limbs were still troubling him after having been tied and motionless throughout the coldest part of the small hours. Arnie, who had brought him to the camp looked almost as morose as the outlaw looked.

Blevins handed over that tobacco sack he had made his smoke from and when Murray took it and half turned so that his eyes would not even inadvertently go to those two dead men again, Jim said, "Whose idea was it, raiding the Mex ranch?"

Arch did not hesitate, but neither did he lift his eyes as he answered. "Toke's. He'd been down in that coun-

try last year when the law was too hot
for him up here. He worked for that
old cowman, got to know all about the
place." Arch lit up and blew smoke
but still would not lift his head.
"Gawddamn," he muttered softly.
"An' we could have made it too. Jake
was right, we could have made it
plumb up through here and out of the
south desert. Could have been home
free."

Arden cocked his head. "Except for
what?"

"That damned woman," stated the
outlaw. "Jake was plumb right and I
didn't even think he could be. He was
doggoned right." Finally, Arch raised
his grey and bristly countenance.
"Where is she?"

"Got away," the saddle-maker said,
still mopping at dripping eyes. "Eh,
Sheriff?"

Blevins shrugged. "For now anyway." He looked around. They could
not carry it all, the loot, the dead men,

the captive, on their own stock plus one more head so he said for them to mount up and later he'd come back from town.

Arch Murray rode behind the sheriff's cantle and as a precaution Jim emptied his hip-holster and shoved the colt down the front of his trousers.

"How did Toke talk Deuce Farragut into going along with you fellers?" he asked his captive, and got a disillusioned-sounding reply.

"They been friends a long while. He snuck in here every now and then and seen her. They was sort of lovers I'd guess you'd call it. Have been for a couple years."

"Did Toke know about her husband?"

"Sure. A feller like Toke Mailer don't run no risks. He figures all the odds in advance, and this time when he wanted her along he even figured out a way for her to get rid of her husband."

"*He* figured that, or *she* did?"

"He did, Sheriff, and then he sat around the campfire tellin' us how he worked that out. Showed Deuce how to drive a sharp rock between the horse's sole and the shoe. It'll lame them every time but usually not for an hour or two."

Blevins killed his smoke atop the horn and pitched it away. Even if he had felt like talking some more this confirmation of his suspicions would have squelched it. But as a matter of fact he was dull from exertion, from long hours under stress, and from killing a man, so now he dogged along looking ahead and saying nothing.

They had a long ride ahead but there was no doubt of their ability to reach Muletown before evening. It crossed Blevins's mind that instead of returning for the loot and the *alforjas* himself, he could hire someone from the liverybarn to go up there in a wagon.

Otherwise he had one unresolved difficulty, and maybe that should have troubled him but it did not, and even when he finally had town in sight, he still did not dwell upon the chances a fresh posse might have of finding Deuce Farragut.

Arch Murray was worried when they got close enough to see rooftops and storefronts as they angled inland from over the north-westerly desert. He muttered something about the Mexicans sending up someone for him.

Blevins knew how that worked; he'd been through it a hundred times down the years. First, there had to be an extradition order issued, then it had to be cleared by both the Mex and U.S. governments, then it had to be returned to the south desert with proper signatures and addenda.

"You've got at least six months," he told Murray, not especially out of pity although it was a known fact that very very few long-termers ever came out alive from a Mex jail or prison, but because he thought it might make the waiting a little easier. He did not really have anything against Arch Murray. The other two were different, particularly Jake Kandelin. Murray had seemed right from the beginning to be the least deadly and venomous of the lot.

They entered town from out back at a time when many people were at supper. Even the liveryman was not there although a dayman was and when Blevins with his possemen rode in looking glum, saying nothing, filthy and villainous-looking, the dayman did exactly what was expected of him right up until he had to loosen the lasso ropes holding the corpses, then he paled and looked around for either assistance or guidance. The possemen went over and dutifully unloaded both corpses and pulled Murray to the ground also, without saying a single word. The dayman looked to Jim Blevins as though he might faint.

Their animals were in better shape than the men. Even the Mexican horse which Blevins told the dayman to stall, cuff, feed, and look after until it was decided what to do about him.

They went up the empty sidewalk to Blevins's jailhouse before anyone saw them and paid much attention, then a rawboned older woman stared, and fled among the houses out back of Main Street, and a slightly inebriated swamper from the saloon looked, made absolutely certain what he had seen by staring until the jailhouse door closed, then he too fled, but his destination was concerned less with gossip than it was over the prospect of cadging a free shot of old popskull for giving the barman a very special bit of gossip.

Inside the sheriff's office for the second time recently, Arnold Ferguson leaned upon a booted carbine and said,

"I got a business to run, y'know, and I figure I've done my bounden duty."

Blevins remembered this discussion before and his promise about it. "I'll scratch your name off the list, Arnie, and I'm right obliged."

Ferguson picked up the saddleboot and walked out into the late day bound tiredly in the direction of his store. The saddle-maker left next, heading up for Doctor Colendar's place to have his eyes looked at. The last of them to depart was Cliff Arden and he was in no hurry so they sat for a while, the prisoner, the sheriff, and the gunsmith, talking quietly as though they were old friends.

Murray was a companionable kind of man. Blevins had already made up his mind on that score long ago. When the prisoner said, "What's the charge?" Blevins made a tired attempt to soften it.

"Depends on what the Mex government does, but I'd guess murder and grand theft for openers."

"What else could there be?" asked the worried man. "Illegally entering the country, horsetheft." Blevins studied the younger man's face. Murray had coarse features but he was not a fool. "It was damned dumb, the three of you going down there."

"Maybe," conceded the captive, "but we got over the line without getting caught didn't we?"

"And that's where the honeymoon ended," said Blevins dryly. "Maybe by the time this thing is all settled up for, you may wish it had ended differently for you."

Murray stared. "Gettin' shot like Toke and——?"

Blevins yawned. "Go on up to your store," he told the gunsmith. "I'm going to lock this one up then head for bed myself."

Murray would not be put off this easily. After Arden had left he said,

"What did you mean I might wish it had ended different?"

Blevins was not in an argumentative frame of mind. He took the key, unlocked the cell-room door, was instantly met by a blast of profanity from Farragut which he totally ignored but which made Murray jump, opened a cell and pushed. Then he closed the door and locked it, all without speaking a word. He then turned, walked down where he could look in on Farragut and said, "I told you, Lee, you were a dumb damned fool. While I'm gone to get your supper ask the feller up the aisle what I meant."

Farragut was furious. "I don't give a damn what you said—you know how long it's been since I've eat anything? Blevins, I'm going to find out if the law can treat a man like this. You got no business lockin' a man in then deliberately not feedin' him so's he'll be weak as a kitten when you come along with your club and chain and all!"

Jim weathered each successive blast with the same stoic expression and when Farragut had to pause to haul down fresh breath Blevins said, "Your wife was with the renegades we chased. That one up yonder is the only one came back alive. Talk to him, Lee."

Blevins walked back to the office, tiredly tossed aside the keys and proceeded over to the Mex cafe for food. He ate in solemn silence ignoring each greeting tossed his way. When he finished he took two trays back across the road with him, and this time when he opened the cell-room door there was not a sound from Leland Farragut.

Blevins fed Arch Murray first, saw the worried look on Murray's face, and went down to the other occupied cell.

Leland sat hunched upon the edge of his bunk and seemed to have gone

deaf when Blevins opened the door
and put the tray inside, called him and
relocked the door. Farragut still sat
staring across at the long, very thin
barred window set into the thick wall.

Blevins went back up to Murray's
cell. "You told him?"

Murray had. "He didn't have no
idea, Sheriff. How can a man live with
a woman and not even suspect anything?"

"You ever been married, Murray?"

"No."

"Then you don't know much about
it?"

"You know his wife, though."

"What's that got to do with it?
Yeah, I know her. And him. And all I
can say is what I've been telling him—
he's a damned fool."

"That's a hell of a thing to tell a
feller when he's just found out
something like this."

"Murray, it's a hell of a thing to tell
a man *any* time at all. I did it because

it seemed to me it'd be better comin' a little at a time, other than just once like a big dose of salts. But hell, I was guessing."

"Tell you one thing, Sheriff. Good thing Toke's dead."

Blevins shrugged. Unless something special happened, like a miracle, it wouldn't make much difference whether Mailer was alive or dead because that damned fool down yonder was going to prison for many years.

This thought reminded Blevins of something. He locked the cell-room door after himself, looked for the hat he had jettisoned after entering the jailhouse, picked it off a chair-seat and went out.

The day was close to ending. John Colendar was out back under an old tree reading his Bible. He was doing this while smoking an evil black Mexican cigar, the only kind men could keep on hand unless they were rich enough to import American stogies and no one fitted that category at Muletown.

The doctor glanced up, chewed a moment on his frayed stogie, gently closed the Bible and set it aside as he kicked a chair around and said, "Sit down, Jim. You look worse'n a desperado. Well; the others told me all about it. Now what?"

"Before I rode out someone told me there was a circuit rider heading our way."

While Blevins eased down and shoved back his hat, then unconsciously put a hand inside his shirt where the hurt was, Colendar was speaking.

"Feller had malaria when he was young. Came from down south somewhere. I think he said it was Alabama. He was sick as a hound dog by the time he got here from Springville. I got him able to navigate and stuffed him in a coach and sent him home." Colendar smiled ruefully. "There went your judge for Lee Farragut. They're strapped he told me. Maybe won't get another one down here for a month ... What are you doing? What's wrong with your chest? Here; put your hand down and lean back. Damn it, stop acting like a child and be still while I ... What the hell happened to you? This feels like ... Jim; get up and come inside to the examination room."

Blevins did not argue but once they were inside and he was ordered to shed his shirt he said, "Doc, I haven't been near a cake of soap and water in a long while."

John Colendar was not put off. "I've smelt boars before," he growled, motioning the lawman to climb onto the examination table. "Take a breath. Can't take a deeper one, eh? What happened, Jim?"

"Horse caught me in the brisket with his knee, I think. Anyway he sure rolled the hell out of me when he went over."

"Yes indeed, I'd say he did bowl you over. That is a separation. You've got several ribs separated from the sternum—from your brisket bone." Colendar stepped back and tapped lightly, listened, tapped some more, put aside his cigar and using both hands worked the muscles until Jim flinched in spite of himself then the older man stepped back and leaned upon a cabinet gazing at the lawman. "You think you're made of iron do you?"

"John; it happened up where the fight took place. I couldn't have done anything different than I did if I'd wanted to."

Colendar sighed and plugged the cigar back between worn, big teeth. "You want a tight bandage?"

"No."

"All right. For that kind of injury it's just something I do because I don't know anything better to do. But all you need, Jim, is another horse-kick or whatever it was, another damned hard blow there and you'll spend the rest of your life in pain every time it rains or every time you want to lift something. Go to bed and stay there for a few days ... I know, I know. You're not going to do it and I know that for a darned fact, but in my trade there are certains things we got to do to keep our own consciences clear. So now I've told you and you'll do what you want to do." Colendar puffed, squinted then said, "Lie back, Jim, I want to do a little more examining. Just lie back, will you—please?" Colendar smiled. "I'll go wash my hands and be right back. Stay up there."

He did not return for a long time, for perhaps as long as fifteen minutes. So long anyway that his cigar was down to a nubbin when he padded silently to the examination room door and looked in.

He smiled. Jim Blevins was sound asleep.

Someone out back banging on the alley door made Colendar curse and whirl to dash back there. He opened the door, glared at the liveryman and his dayman and said, "Confound it do you *always* have to go banging on this door?"

The two men in the yard looked round-eyed. Neither of them had knocked back here before. The liveryman turned and jerked a thumb. "Two corpses in that manure cart, Doctor. Where you want 'em—in the wagon shed across the alley?"

"Yes." Doctor Colendar walked forth, spat out his cigar butt and lifted the soiled horseblanket to peer beneath it. Nothing ever surprised John Colendar and since he had already been told the posseman had returned with a brace of dead renegades he gazed dispassionately at the grey faces, dropped the blanket and turned to the liveryman, who was also older.

"What a senseless waste this sort of thing is. If they are dead-set on doing stupid things and getting themselves killed for it, will you tell me, Emmett, why the good Lord in all His wisdom didn't fix it so's decent law-abiding older fellers like you and me couldn't somehow cut them open, remove the unspent years and transplant them?"

The liveryman was an individual of great knowledge about horses and mules, a litle knowledge about harness and saddlery, a little knowledge of humanity too, but this time he was stopped in his tracks by an idea which had never before come to his mind.

Doctor Colendar jerked his thumb towards the shed across the alley and walked back into the house, closing the door very gently. Behind him the dayman scratched vigorously, waited for his employer to get over whatever was holding him like a wooden Indian so they could get shed of the dead and get back down the alley where there was feeding and watering to be done.

Overhead, the sky gradually darkened, the same pale old stars which had been viewing human frailty, stupidity, apathy and grandeur since the Very Beginning, were just now starting to show a little light again.

14

SHADOWS

There were probably more than two kinds of rest, but not in the insular, simple environment of the south desert where men either slept well, in proper beds and with moderately clear consciences, or there was the kind of rest Jim Blevins got which had to do exclusively with being exhausted and worn out so that a man could sleep soundly for hours on end upon a hard wooden examination table.

The result, when men awakened from both categories, was very different. Jim opened both eyes, considered the dimly lighted star-washed ceiling, wondered where he was, remembered, and started to rise up.

The pain in his chest came back so he rolled slightly and using one arm, levered himself into a sitting position first, then into a standing position as he felt for his shirt and put it on slowly enough to permit him to make the full transition not only from his jailhouse office to John Colendar's examination room, but also from day to full night.

He went to the window, cocked an eye at a slumbering dark and silent town, turned with a yawn and scratched, then found his hat and headed forth into the waiting-room. It was empty too, slightly chilly and in this poor reflected light from outside it looked a little worn and threadbare.

He smelled coffee and went ploughing through until he found John Colendar in the kitchen, freshly shaved, bright-eyed and making breakfast. The doctor turned, studied Jim for a moment, then grinned as he said, "Good morning; I've never seen you look so disreputable. There's a razor and wash-water out back on the porch if you'd care——"

"What time is it, John?"

Colendar went through all the motions of drawing his watch, opening the face and looking downward. Then he shoved the watch over. "See for yourself. Five o'clock."

Blevins stared at John Colendar and ignored the watch. "Five—in the morning?"

Colendar pocketed his watch and turned back to flip eggs and look in the oven to see if the toast was golden-brown yet. It was, so he flipped it upon a wooden drainboard where a sturdy little butter firkin stood, and blew briefly upon his fingers.

"Yeah—five in the morning. You slept, by my calculation, just exactly ten hours." Colendar looked around. "You can butter the toast, or I'll do that and you can go out back and wash. On second thought, you go wash and *I'll* butter the toast."

Blevins went dutifully to the rear door, considered John for a moment, then shook his head and went out to the washrack.

There was a chill in the air, off towards the far-away east the sun was just coming along, sending in advance its skyward hoard of raw pale gold; closer in there was almost no sound yet although surely most of Muletown's inhabitants were rousing.

Southward down the alley where shadows lingered longest, he could see the back of his jailhouse as he shaved with Calendar's wicked-bladed straight razor. His chest ached, his back ached from lying asleep for so long on that wooden examination table, and yet he could ruefully smile at the freshly-shaved, shiny countenance in the wash-rack mirror. John Colendar was not just unique, he was *good*. Not nice-good nor simply pleasant-good like people were who did things so that other people would be impressed by their goodness, John Colendar was good in his rough, understanding, caring way. And that, in Blevins's view was the best way to make it in this life.

He went inside and his friend motioned. Their food was equally divided upon plates at the table, the kitchen smelled wonderfully of hot coffee, it was warm, and suddenly Sheriff Jim was as hungry as a bitch wolf at whelping time, so he sat and dived in.

For a while they said nothing, just ate and drank coffee, but eventually John had the same question Blevins had been asked the day before.

"What about Deuce?"

Jim looked up slowly. "I hope she makes it."

"To where?"

"Damned if I know, John. Just out of my territory."

"On foot in the desert, Jim?"

"Any way that she can."

Colendar sipped coffee and gazed upon the evenly tanned strong face opposite him. "What about Leland?"

"That damned fool," exclaimed the sheriff. "That stupid idiotic darned simpleton!" Blevins's exasperation boiled over in the first explanation he had given anyone up to this time of how he really felt about Farragut.

"You can't rob a stage, not even half way, and not get the book thrown at you. In the Territory folks are extra sensitive about some crimes, and stage-robbery is one of them. Deuce and her lover that dead feller named Toke Mailer, set Lee up and she went right along and made damned sure he'd have a lame horse, and that I'd have a shot posseman. John, you can't get a worse set of circumstances against a highwayman than that. ... He'll go to prison as sure as I'm setting here and maybe for one hell of a long time, and why? Because he was thick as oak."

"Is it being thick to trust your wife, Jim?"

"That's the part that sticks in my throat, John."

"Anything you can do?"

Jim reached for the cup of coffee. "Yeah; I can plead like a Dutch uncle at his trial, and after they convict him, which sure as hell they'll do, I can take it on for a couple of years maybe and write letters, call on judges, make life miserable for everyone until I can get him out on probation or parole."

"Will you do it?"

"Yes, I'll do it. But do you know what else I'd like to do? Kick him as hard as I can right in the——"

"Someone's out front at the door," exclaimed Doctor Colendar, putting aside his cup and getting heavily to his feet. "If there's anything to this reincarnation thing, Jim, don't be a doctor the next time around. Finish your breakfast."

Two minutes after John Colendar

had departed and just as Sheriff
Blevins was indeed finishing his meal,
the doctor appeared in the doorway
looking distraught as he curtly said,
"You better come with me."

Blevins knew that expression on the
human face. He arose without a
question and stepped around the table.
Out in the waiting-room there were
three rangemen looking grave and concerned. Jim recognised only one of
them and nodded to him.

"Morning, Buff, how's the shoulder?"

Rhodes replied by moving the arm
gingerly, but moving it.

Jim passed on through the adjoining
door and stopped dead in his tracks.
Over in the same bed Buff Rhodes had
languished in only a short while ago,
Deuce Farragut lay still and pale in
the fresh morning window-light.

Colendar went to the bedside and
leaned, then stepped slightly to one

side as Jim Blevins finally found himself and came on up.

The woman did not open her eyes, speak nor move. She seemed to scarcely be breathing and Jim raised his eyes to John Colendar's face.

The doctor was as forthright as he usually was, even in front of patients except that this time it did not matter.

"Unconscious," he said. "Harry went across to the store to fetch me some stuff I'll need. He and a couple of his men found her this morning about dawn." Colendar paused to reassess the still grey face. "Found her lying behind a corral at the cow-camp. Harry thinks she was trying to steal one of his horses. She had a lariat and a bridle."

"But what happened to her?"

Doc lifted one side of the blankets. Deuce's entire lower right side, above the hip and higher, was badly swollen and puffily discoloured. Jim had never seen such an extensive wound before. Doctor Colendar lowered the blankets.

"Rattlesnake bite."

Blevins had seen those before, any number of times. "Why is her entire body purple and swollen? I've seen——"

"I'm sure you have, Jim. We all have. But not in the soft parts. Usually folks are bitten in the leg or maybe even the hand or arm. I'd guess she was perhaps down on all fours for some reason and didn't see this one until it struck. Anyway, even if someone had been handy to make a twist above the bite—this time there would have been no way. She took the full force of that venom right into her entrails. Into her stomach and maybe more directly into other organs." Doctor Colendar turned from the bed towards the sheriff. "Her chances in my estimate are blessed slim. Anyway, I'm going to go to work on her now, if you'll help me pack her into the examination room, then leave and take Harry Horton's riders with you."

Ten minutes later Jim Blevins stood with his back to the closed door listening to Buff Rhodes say, "I never in my life seen anything like that. Did you?"

He was the only cowboy still in the waiting-room. The others had evidently gone out to care for the horses or perhaps to meet Harry Horton across at the general store.

Blevins said, "Who found her?"

"I did. Me'n Harry went down to the corral because the horses had been actin' spooked last night every now and then, like they'll do when maybe there's a skunk or badger or some little mean critter around. Harry went one way. I went out back to start looking—and hell's bells there was Deuce Farragut lying cold and unconscious clutching a lariat and a bridle and lookin' like she'd been runnin' and hidin' for a day or two. Even if she'd been standin' up she would have shocked hell out'n me."

"Who figured out she'd been snake-bit?"

"Harry," said the cowboy, and as though mention of his name were a cue the wiry, leathery cowman entered through a blast of soundless golden sun-brightness as the door opened, and stepped in with packages in both arms to kick the door closed with a boot-heel while gazing at the lawman.

Horton said, "I just been talkin' to Arnie over at the store. I didn't have no idea you went out with a posse nor that those renegades who raided down in Sonora had been caught and kil-led."

Doc had evidently heard and recognised the rancher's voice. He appeared in the doorway frowning and holding out his hands. Harry Horton went over, handed across the packages and as Doc stepped back without even a 'thank you' and closed the door

Harry faced Jim again. He sighed,
wagged his head and went back to sit
in a rickety old cane-bottomed chair.
"Darndest snakebite I ever saw. You
see it, Jim?"

Blevins crossed to the roadside door,
opened it and jerked his head for
Buffie Rhodes to leave. Both Buff and
his employer reacted with surprise,
and Buff even showed a little resent-
ment, but he walked out. After Blevins
closed the door he said, "It was her
shot him, Harry." When Horton
looked blank he said, "Deuce Farragut,
not Leland, shot Buff off his saddle
when we rode out to fetch Leland
back. She was in the rocks with him."

The hard and weathered cowman
said, "Ah hell, Jim ... Are you
absolutely sure?"

"Yeah, I'm sure."

Horton considered his outthrust
scuffed boot-toes. "I'll be gawddam-
ned. In the rocks too? None of the
other posse-fellers I've talked to knew

that. They sure as the devil never said nothin' to me about it." Horton turned a screwed-up forehead above doubting pale eyes. "Are you *dead* sure?"

"Dead sure. It's a long story. Leland—well—she and a man named Toke Mailer, one of those raiders who hit the Mex ranch, schemed to set Leland up, lame his horse, and have an accident happen to one of the possemen. That took Leland out of it for her—and her latest lover."

Horton stared, head slightly to one side as though at least some of his scepticism lingered.

"Those Mex *vaqueros* still at your camp?" asked the sheriff, then explained his reason for asking. "We got the loot back, including the pouches of gold coins. If they'll get word to the *ranchero* down yonder, why he can send up someone or come himself, identify the stuff, and take it back with him."

Horton was nodding over all this,

but when he spoke again his thoughts were still clearly upon Deuce's perfidy. "Arnie said she was leaving the country with them renegades."

That had to be purest conjecture. Probable, but not yet something which could be proved, so Blevins turned it aside with a brief comment.

"Maybe. She's the only one can answer that. Anyway ..."

Doctor Colendar came to the door, poked out his head to ignore the cowman and say, "Jim—in here please."

Blevins had a bad feeling as he arose to cross the room.

Deuce had been covered with a cotton sheet, her head propped slightly upon a little white matching pillow. she looked slightly flushed and her eyes were brighter than usual, but they were steady and rational in their regard of Sheriff Blevins as she hoarsely said, "Where's Leland? Still in your jailhouse?"

Jim nodded and came closer to the

table while Doctor Colendar went to a cupboard with his back to them.

"Toke … ?"

"Dead. Him and Jake Kandelin," replied Blevins. "Arch is in one of my cells."

"Leland knows?" she asked, and again Jim nodded his head. "All of it, Sheriff; everything?"

"I told him some, Deuce, and Arch told him the rest of it." He leaned and found her hand, slipped strong fingers around her fingers and held tightly.

She looked briefly away, then back. "Sheriff … I'm going out … Will you hold me like that?"

Blevins softly smiled. "Sure. Always did sort of want to hold your hand."

"No, you never did. You hated my guts. You never had one lick of use for me and you know it."

Blevins had no intention of lying to her, particularly at this point in her existence, so he turned her accusation aside with a little squeeze and a wink.

"You could have just given up, surrendered to us yesterday, Deuce."

"And be brought back here for everyone to know what I did? Sheriff Blevins, I wanted a horse, that was all, and a little headstart. That was all. I know a town over in northern New Mexico ..."

Jim waited, clinging warmly to her fingers still, and after a while, still clinging, he turned and said, "John ..."

Colendar came over and leaned. In a soft version of his usual crisp self he said, "That's it."

Blevins raised her hand and gently laid it across her chest. He could not swallow and the little room was suddenly far too confining.

Colendar looked around and for a moment simply watched his friend before saying, "I've done this more than you have. Want me to go tell Leland he's a widower?"

Jim went to the door before answering. "No. I'll tell him, John ... Damn; so darned silly and pointless."

Colendar did not change expression. "Glad you noticed. I say that every time I get one like this—man or woman. What in the tarnation hell sense does it make; you're only here for a very short length of time under the best of conditions, so what sense does it make to deliberately take the kind of chances that will eventually get you killed ... Jim?"

"I'm goin' over to my office and sleep for a little while, then I'll be over at the barbershop using the bathhouse, and after that I'll eat ... Then I'll tell Leland." He looked one final time at the still, handsome face of the dead woman, then with a bitter twisting of the heart yanked open the door and walked out.

Harry Horton spoke from his chair. Blevins went past and out into the golden morning sunlight leaving Harry gaping. Colendar stood in his examination room doorway until after the sheriff was gone, then he said, "She died, Harry. And you could do us all a favour—just leave Jim Blevins alone. Keep out of his way at least until tomorrow. That goes for Buff and the rest of them."

Horton was not an unfeeling man, but he had never been more than superficially involved with women so now he tried to silently puzzle through Colendar's imputation that Deuce's death had cut deeply into the lawman who knew best of all what she had been and who could certainly not have liked nor respected her for it.

He sat a moment gazing at the yonder wall, then slapped his legs and arose. "All right. I got plenty work on the range without hanging around here. Doc ...?"

"Yeah."

"What about Leland?"

Colendar knew only as much as Blevins had told him and he had over the years made a special point of avoiding involvement in things like this, even when the temptation to philosophise was strong, so now he went across the room to hold the door open for Horton, then said, "I don't understand about two-thirds of the things I've seen in this life, Harry. All I try to do is ameloriate as many of the bad ones as I can, and mind my own business."

Horton walked on out, resettled his hat on the porch before striking out in the direction of the saloon. It was early in the morning, for a fact, but he had just seen two of his riders enter over there.

Doc did not return to the examination room right away. He closed the door as gently as though she were sleeping, and walked over to the dark and littered little office where the back-wall window overlooking his rear garden showed flowers and sunlight and tree-shade with birds flashing in and out, fished for a Mex stogie in a desk drawer, lit the thing then stepped to the window, hands clasped, to think for the thousandth time that unless there was some kind of sequential order in things, life just did not make one damned bit of sense.